Destined

NEW HEIGHTS PUBLISHING
www.suzannefalter.com

Book cover design by Caroline Manchoulas
www.ladylit.com

Book design by Danielle H. Acee
www.authorsassistant.com

ISBN: 978-0-9969981-5-4

Destined

An Oaktown Girls Novel

by

SUZANNE **FALTER**

For Teal,
who loved the Goddesses

Chapter One

An alarm sounding like a waterfall began its soothing whoosh. It was followed by the tinkling of bamboo chimes.

"Wha—?" Frankie was suddenly woken out of a sound stupor.

Sally was already moving silently around the bedroom. "Go back to sleep," she whispered, giving her phone a tap to silence the alarm.

Frankie yawned and rolled on her back, and smiled at her lover's extremely typical alarm. "What time is it?"

"Just past four."

Frankie had been asleep for exactly two hours. But then, that was life when you worked a night shift, and across the bay in San Francisco, no less. She studied Sally moving around in the half-light. Her naked body was rounded and ripe, like a beautiful piece of fruit. As she studied her lover, she became aware of something.

Frankie was actually going to miss Sally—even if she was only giving her roommates a ride to the airport.

Sleeping together after Frankie's shift ended a few nights a week had become something of a ritual for them in the six months since they'd begun dating. And now Sally was being plucked out of bed by her large heart, plus a sense of duty to her friends.

Frankie rolled over. *Get a grip*, she cautioned herself. Sally would undoubtedly reappear and then climb back in bed, ready to begin again. For that was another amazing thing about Sally. She loved sex—and lots of it.

Frankie watched Sally fasten the last few buttons of her blouse and regard herself in the mirror. Tentatively, Sally stabbed at her fluffy, ash-blonde hair. Then she glanced over at Frankie. "Go back to sleep, honey," she said. "It's okay."

Frankie smiled. "I like watching you."

Sally smiled back, and stepped into her jeans. She zipped them up, pulled on a baggy sweater and stuffed her feet into her sneakers. "I'll be back in…what…hour and a half?"

"By then the sun will be up," Frankie commented.

"Yeah, but don't leave, okay?"

"Don't worry," Frankie smiled as she closed her eyes. "I'm not going anywhere."

There was a gentle tap at the bedroom door. It was Tenika. "You up, Sally?"

"Almost ready," she called. Then she bent over, her mouth only inches away from Frankie's. "Bye," she said. "I love you."

"Drive carefully," Frankie replied. "Make sure you're awake. Lower a window. Text me from SFO."

"Honey—please. Go back to sleep."

"Okay," said Frankie with a tired sigh. She didn't need to micromanage Sally's safety. She just forgot sometimes. It was all that police training. "Bye."

Still, she couldn't resist. "Don't text me—call me!" she yelled as Sally slipped through the door.

What was she doing?

Frankie gave another heavy sigh and rolled over. She did what she'd been doing ever since she'd been with the SFPD. She was worrying excessively about everyone and everything around her. Though, yes, the scant bit of therapy she'd done had slowed that impulse down.

Slightly. Now she just had PTSD Lite instead of the full-on variety.

Closing her eyes, Frankie once again waited for sleep as she listened to Tenika and her new wife, Delilah, roll their suitcases past the bedroom door. "You got the passports? You're sure?" she heard Tenika ask. She missed Delilah's barely coherent reply.

Frankie yawned. *I love you,* Sally had said as she leaned in for a kiss. Sally said that a lot. Way more than Frankie, that was for sure. In fact, Frankie had yet to say those three critical words to Sally.

It wasn't just that she wasn't ready. It was more that Frankie was conflicted. On one hand, Sally was one of the most gentle, openhearted people Frankie had ever met. Her simple, sweet innocence was pure, and her view of life unclouded. Being with her was like a fresh splash of sunshine all over Frankie's life.

Honestly, this undid Frankie a little. After all, in her work she spent her days following up on people's worst instincts, and suspecting everyone of everything. This was the life of an under-cover cop. She seldom, if ever, got to spend time with people who were just plain good. The other officers in her squad were mostly decent-hearted people. But the perps were…well, perps. You basically spent your days suspecting people of things.

So, yes, it was true. In Frankie's world, Sally was unique. A true gift at a time when she needed it most. If it wasn't for the fact that Sally was a professional psychic, Frankie would already be thinking long-term relationship.

The metaphysical psychic thing stopped Frankie cold. Which was why she'd told exactly no one at work about her girlfriend, and how she could read people's minds and see their futures. She hadn't taken Sally to drinks or dinners with the guys on the force. She hadn't even told the women at the station about her.

Frankie was just plain embarrassed. The minute any of them found out about it, the razzing would never stop. She could see it now. They'd all start trying to levitate in front of her. Or someone would show up at a party in a turban like the Amazing Kreskin.

One way or another, a price would be paid.

Frankie's professional reputation was now officially on the line, as well. Twice she'd been written up in the last six months for erratic outbursts. And so, Frankie was now backpedaling furiously, trying to save her once sterling reputation from the ravages of her own PTSD.

Not only was the condition never discussed in the department, it was also looked down upon. A sign of weakness, as it were. Even though, one way or another, everyone seemed to have it.

Rolling over once more, Frankie clamped her eyes shut and tried hard to go back to sleep in Sally's bed. As she did, she considered the delights that awaited when Sally returned.

With a smile, she once again began to nod off. Sally would be back before she knew it.

*

Tenika gazed out at the line of traffic that snaked ahead. It was a sea of red lights between them and SFO's international terminal. "Damn," she said. "What are all these people doing here, anyway? It's four-thirty in the frigging morning!"

"Honey, we still have nearly three hours," Delilah commented from the backseat.

"It'll be okay," said Sally, her hands tightening on the wheel as she sped up. "Look—it's already breaking up."

"Yeah. Whatever," Tenika sighed. Racing to an airport in the pre-dawn darkness went against everything in her system, especially the idea that when they finally got there they'd have to rush. Tenika was a lover of order, of calm. Of everything being in its right place, at the right time.

"So what's this place called you're going to again?" Sally asked.

"Glover's Reef," Tenika said. "It's a tiny island, thirty miles off the coast of Belize. No electricity. No Internet. No traffic. No nothing, basically, except a whole lot of snorkeling and fishing. It's just us in our little grass hut over the water. Us and the manta rays for two whole weeks."

"Sounds incredible," Sally remarked.

"Yep," Tenika asserted. Reaching back, she gave her new wife's hand a squeeze. "Anyway, how many honeymoons are we going to go on? Sometimes you just have to blow the savings; you know what I'm saying?"

Tenika and Delilah had just been married a few days earlier, among San Francisco City Hall's soaring marble colonnades and archways. A justice of the peace married them in front of a handful of friends.

Lizzy, Tenika's business partner, had been the witness, while Sally served as the maid of honor, handing over the ring at the right moment. Delilah wore a vintage fifties white cocktail dress with a flared organza skirt, and Tenika sported a rented tux, her long, thin braids spilling down her back in a shiny black cascade.

There was silence for a moment as they inched along. Delilah finally spoke up. "Sally, don't you have that interview today?"

Sally glanced at her old friend in the rear-view mirror. "Yeah," she said lightly, as a little clench of fear gripped her gut. "In six hours, actually," she replied, glancing at the clock on the dashboard.

"Don't worry, hon," Delilah soothed. "You're going to do great."

"Hell, yeah!" Tenika added. "I mean—whoever that chick is, she'd be lucky to have you."

"Thanks," Sally said. "But, I don't know…" Her voice trailed off.

"Don't know what?" Tenika asked. "If you're good enough? You're good enough, Sally. Hella good enough."

"Yeah, I mean, Sally—when are you wrong? Like…ever?" Delilah added.

"I've just never done this before. Professionally, I mean. It's a big deal, agreeing to read for total strangers. What if I get someone in there and I choke? What if the cards are totally screwy, or what if I choke and I can't read them? What if I say the wrong

13

thing?" Her voice ratcheted up in the darkness. "These people will be paying me!"

Tenika laughed beside her. "You got this," she said.

Sally stared out at the still stalled headlights in front of her, and she sighed. "But I have to do it," she reasoned more quietly. "I know I do."

"You're damn right," Tenika said.

Delilah leaned forward emphatically. "You are a psychic, Sally. This is what you do. This is who you are."

The three of them were silent for a moment.

"Thanks," Sally finally said. Then she smiled over at Tenika. "What are we going to do while you two are gone? T, has Lizzy ever even run the garage alone?" Tenika and her business partner, Lizzy, owned an automotive garage in Oakland. Driven was Woman Powered, Woman Owned, as the sign out front put it.

"Hey, don't forget our history. Lizzy's the one who stepped in when I broke my arm back in the day. She'll be fine," Tenika said. Finally, the car picked up more speed as the traffic jam began to break up. "Anyway, it's good for her to run things alone for a while, you know? Get her up to speed on the rest of the business."

Moments later, Sally pulled up to the curb and parked. "Okay, ladies. You have arrived," she said as she swung out of the driver's seat.

"Just call us if you guys need anything," Delilah said, pulling her suitcase from the back. "I left the phone number on the kitchen counter."

"It's just a landline," Tenika added. "There's no cell service or anything. Anyway, I'm sure you won't even need it. What could possibly go wrong?"

Sally didn't answer as a swarm of possibilities filled her head. As if reading her mind, Tenika patted her arm. Then she reached over to give Sally a long hug. "Come on, sis. You're going to do fine. Everyone is. Don't worry!

"Totally fine," Delilah added, unsnapping the handle from her roller bag and pulling it up. Holding out her arms, she hugged Sally. They'd known each other since college, and the bond had held fast for some years now. "And like I said, just call us if you need anything at all."

"We're only a phone call—and an ocean—away!" Tenika added jauntily. She grabbed her suitcase from the back and spun around toward the terminal, her long braids flying. *"Man,* am I ready for this trip," she announced. "Paradise, here we come!"

"Have a blast! And don't worry," Sally called.

"Who's worrying? You're worrying," Tenika remarked over her shoulder. Then she gave a wave as she and Delilah disappeared into the international terminal. Taking a deep breath, Sally put the car in drive and pulled out. As she did, her mind now turned to the next task before her: the interview.

But first, there was Frankie. And her warm, waiting bed.

Chapter Two

Kate gave her long, strawberry blonde hair a final brush and regarded herself in her bathroom mirror. She turned this way and that, checking the edge of her top and pulling on a loose thread, making sure everything was just so.

Lizzy stood in the doorway, gazing at her lover. "You look nice today," she said.

Kate smiled at Lizzy as she snapped off the light. "Thank you, love. Now let's go."

Lizzy was always one to linger at such moments, and today Kate had things to do. She was eager to get on with her day. "Have to get to Berkeley and back before ten."

Her Irish accent made Berkeley sound like 'Bark-lee,' and it made Lizzy smile. Kate's gentle accent was just one of the many touchstones that Lizzy relied on, day after day, in the happy thrall of their still-developing relationship.

Lizzy followed Kate into the kitchen, grabbing her lunch kit as she passed on her way to the front door. She tucked it into her backpack and zipped it up.

"Do you want a ride to work?" Kate asked.

"Nope. I have my bike with me...remember? But thanks." Lizzy pulled open the apartment door and unlocked her bike from its spot in the hallway outside Kate's apartment. Hoisting it over her shoulder, she began to make her way down the stairs to the street.

Lizzy waited for Kate to come outside as she put on her helmet.

"I think I'll drop by the garage today," Kate said airily, as she locked the front door. "Given that you'll be alone and such."

Lizzy stopped short and looked at her girlfriend. Immediately she began shaking her head. "No, no, no, no, no... Honey. *Please.*"

"What?" Kate asked innocently.

"Oh, baby, come on! What about ICE?" Lizzy's worst fear was that Immigration and Customs Enforcement would suddenly show up at the garage, where Kate had been unofficially working part-time for several months. They'd pull out their handcuffs, and that would be that. Kate would be gone and their tender, beautiful, steadily improving relationship would basically be over.

"Now come, Lizzy. There's been no sign of trouble for six months now. I'm sure I'm a long forgotten number at the bottom of a file," she insisted. "Besides, now Tenika's off on holiday and you're there alone, I think you need support. I know you do."

Kate had proved immeasurably helpful to Lizzy's business, ever since their relationship began. It was Kate who created the conversation corner, a cozy nook in the garage for local lesbians, especially the single ones, to chat while waiting for their cars. It had proven a success—and an amazingly effective marketing tool.

Lizzy couldn't deny it. Having Kate around always made things run better at Driven.

"Well..." Lizzy began slowly. Then she faltered. "I mean, look," she began. "That's nice and everything, but seriously, Kate. You could get busted any day, so why run the risk? You're much safer working here in your own apartment."

Unexpectedly, Kate laughed. "Now Lizzy, you're making a very large mountain out of a molehill; you know you are. And in case you're forgetting, this will only be my apartment for another week. Then I'll be living at your apartment—or as you like to call it, 'our apartment'." She grinned at her lover in amusement. "Or did you forget?"

Lizzy smiled shyly and looked down at her boots. "No, I didn't forget," she muttered. She glanced up at Kate again, taking in her ice blue eyes and the cleft in her chin and the sheer loveliness of who she was. As usual, her heart gave a small, uncontrollable flip.

"I just couldn't stand it if something happened to you, baby," Lizzy admitted.

"Nothing's going to happen to me. And I am coming by today. And that is that." Leaning over, Kate gave Lizzy a kiss, then another. Then finally a longer one. Kate pulled back an inch. "It will all be just fine," she said. "I know it will."

"Okay. If you say so…" Lizzy said uncertainly as she straddled her bike. She pushed off gently in the direction of her garage. "Bye!" she called over her shoulder.

"And be careful on the bloody bike!" Kate called after her. "Mind the trucks!"

Lizzy gave a wave in response and rode away. Behind her, Kate's car took off in the opposite direction.

Kate.

How could Lizzy begin to describe the cascade of emotions that poured through her body every time she thought about her girlfriend. There was the very fact that they were together, which after the last six months they'd been through seemed remarkable in itself.

First, there had been the rescue phase when Lizzy helped Kate pry herself out of a toxic live/work arrangement with Mindy, her former boss. That move had required all of the strength Kate had, for Mindy's hold on her had been relentless. Immediately, Kate had moved in with Lizzy and began working at the garage, mainly because she needed a safe place to land in a hurry.

Their dating relationship took off like an unmanned rocket— an intoxicating blend of chemistry, lust, and need as they discovered who they were together. Lizzy had simply been too eager, too blown away…and far too engaged in what might lie ahead for them for

Kate to settle in comfortably. The pressure was palpable. Hence the arrival of the *I need space* phase.

That was when Kate had moved out to find her own temporary studio apartment and her own work as a freelance marketing consultant. She had to for the sake of the relationship, she said. Otherwise, they would surely break up. But as Kate lived alone, day by day, she remembered what had brought them together in the first place. The fact was that she missed Lizzy.

Now they were here. The experiment in living apart had worked. The relationship had thrived, and Kate's sublease was almost up. So Kate was poised to move back in with Lizzy. She was ready, she said, to make the commitment that had been so elusive the first time around.

Still, there was the other dark truth that kept lingering around the edges of their happiness, threatening to derail the whole thing. Kate could get deported at any moment. Especially since Mindy, her vengeful former boss, had turned her in to ICE.

Oddly, months later, ICE had yet to do anything about it.

The sad truth was that Kate was an undocumented worker, living illegally in the US, as she had been for the past seven years. The irony was that finally Lizzy had a lover she could count on, and the committed relationship she'd longed for, for years. Simply put, Kate was 'the One.' And now…well, the whole thing could be shot to hell at any moment.

Lizzy pumped along on her bike, up and down the various hills that stood between Kate's apartment and her business, and tried not to think about the whole ICE situation. Her impulse all along had been to keep Kate hidden away. The temporary sublet— the address of which Kate had never registered anywhere—seemed perfect. Presumably, ICE would have a very hard time finding her. Especially since even her former boss had no idea she was there.

But now the sublet was ending, and ICE had yet to surface. But Driven, unfortunately, Mindy knew all about, including the fact that Kate occasionally worked there. Hence, Lizzy's fear she might lose her if Kate showed up at Driven. The knot in her gut hadn't really left since she'd learned that her lover was undocumented.

Yet it seemed a small price to pay for smart, beautiful, light-filled Kate.

Lizzy pulled up to a stoplight and rolled her shoulders, trying to relieve the tension as she waited for it to change. Kate would move back in, and then they'd just have to take their chances. Who knew? Maybe her name really was now lost in a file somewhere.

The light changed, and Lizzy set off once again.

Everything would be fine, Kate had said. And for all Lizzy knew, it was true.

If she could just keep herself from proposing marriage a week after Kate moved in, well…then everything really *would* be fine.

*

"I'm here!" Kate called easily as she came strolling into the garage a few hours later.

Lizzy looked up from the Toyota she was working on. "Hey."

"Oh, what a grand sight—to see you hard at work," Kate continued, giving Lizzy a kiss on her cheek. Her tall, rangy, butch girlfriend was always a sight to behold, standing there in her navy coveralls with a wrench in her hand. Kate especially loved the way Lizzy's short, dark hair curled over the edge of her collar.

"Seems like months since I've been here," she said, turning around to take the place in.

"Yep. And necessarily so," said Lizzy, wiping her hands on a rag.

Kate walked over to the conversation corner, then she glanced back at Lizzy with a smile. "Doesn't look bad at all. You've been keeping it up," she noted. "You even have a fresh pot of coffee on."

"I do what I can," Lizzy said humbly. "Someone's always here these days, hanging out." Kate barely heard Lizzy's remarks as she poked through the tea and coffee supplies. Crouching down, she opened the mini fridge. "Darling, you're out of half-and-half," she said. Then she stood up. "You really can't run out of cream, you know. That's a particularly deadly sin."

"Sounds serious," Lizzy noted dryly. "I'll get some when I go out for lunch."

"If you want to bring in the customers, you need three things—" Kate began, but Lizzy finished her sentence for her as she took her in her arms. "Good coffee and cream, a comfortable, clean place to sit, and something to do. I've got it memorized."

"Excuse me—" Kate and Lizzy suddenly broke apart as an unfamiliar voice joined them.

Turning, they took in the sight of the petite, slender Asian woman standing before them. She had the polished look of a tech geek. A pair of high-end glasses, a collared striped shirt, and expensive black pants completed her look, as did her lizard flats. Behind her was the car she'd just parked, a fairly new Prius. Her long, black hair gleamed in the fluorescent work light of the garage.

"My check engine light just came on. Do you work on hybrids?"

"Sure," said Lizzy, coming toward her with an outstretched hand. "I'd be happy to take a look. I'm Lizzy, by the way."

"Hello," said the young woman, pointedly not sharing her name. She made no effort to shake Lizzy's hand, and after a beat Lizzy put her outstretched hand in her pocket. Still, she smiled gamely at the new customer.

"It's a twenty-seventeen," the woman continued. "It's so weird—it wasn't just check engine that came on. It was all the warning lights, and they came on all at once just as I was driving by. It was kind of freaky to tell you the truth."

"Good timing, I'd say," Lizzy remarked. "But don't worry. I've seen this before. Twenty-seventeen, you said?" The woman nodded, and put her hands on her hips. She had the dumbfounded air of someone who had never had unexpected trouble like this in her entire life.

Lizzy contemplated the vehicle for a moment, then she turned to her customer. "Did you have your car serviced recently? Oil change or anything?"

"Oil change two days ago. You think that was the cause?"

"The twenty-seventeen Prius has some weird quirks in the wiring. I'll take a look. Can you leave it?"

The woman shrugged. "Well, what else am I going to do?"

"Let me see if I can figure this out quickly," Lizzy proposed. In a flash Kate was by the young woman's side.

"Can I get you a cup of coffee, love?" Kate asked. She motioned the woman over to the conversation corner as Lizzy opened the hood of the Prius and set to work behind them. "Terrible nuisance, something like this, isn't it?" Kate said, advancing on the coffee pot. "Here," she said, offering an empty mug. "Have some? We just made a pot."

The young woman didn't say much, but she did warm to the idea of a cup of coffee. "Have a seat. Relax," Kate urged. "You don't take cream, do you?"

"Black's fine." The Asian woman took the coffee and found a seat in the conversation corner.

Kate handed over the steaming mug of coffee. "I'm Kate, by the way."

"Thanks. I'm Rosalind. Rosalind Choi."

Kate smiled at her new friend. "Nice to meet you, Rosalind. Do you live around here?"

Rosalind shook her head. "No. I live on the Embarcadero. I just arrived in Oakland," she said. "Came over from the city when I got a new job here."

"Ah," said Kate. "How are you finding it?"

The young woman glanced around. "Oakland or the job?"

"Any or all of it."

"Oh, it's fine. Oakland, I mean," Rosalind said quickly. An awkward silence followed. Kate was pretty sure Rosalind wasn't finding her new job fine at all.

"Tech?" she asked lightly, and Rosalind nodded. "Must be a tough road, so few women…" Rosalind just smiled blandly and said nothing.

An awkward beat of silence went by. Kate could practically feel the young woman itching to pull out her phone and detach.

"Well, anyway, it's lovely you found your way here," Kate continued. "This is a women's garage, you know. My girlfriend, Lizzy, co-owns it with Tenika Cummins. She's away on her honeymoon, with her new wife, Delilah. A remarkable number of women seem to find each other here. A bit of a miracle, really," she added gently.

"Ah," said Rosalind, with a brief, fake smile. Abruptly, she stood up. "I actually need to go. Is she going to be long?" Rosalind asked.

"At any rate, you've found yourself an excellent mechanic," Kate continued, sensing her discomfort. "Highly rated on Yelp and all that. She'll get you fixed up in no time, I'm sure."

As if on cue, Lizzy shut the hood of the Prius and came walking in their direction. Rosalind moved toward her expectantly, eager to have clarity and move on.

"There's a fan issue," Lizzy said as she reached her. "Some debris must have gotten kicked up by the oil change. I'm afraid I have to replace the fan."

"Replace it!"

"Like I said, the twenty-seventeens are tweaky. The good news is I can get one in just a few days. But you will have to leave the car in the meantime. It can't be driven."

Rosalind sighed and glanced at her watch. Then she looked around, her hands once more on her hips, as if taking the measure of the place. "All right," she said uncertainly. "I guess I have no choice. If you're sure we have to replace the fan…"

Lizzy nodded. "Yeah, I'm sorry about that. All kinds of stuff can get in there. Then the rotors burn out, and here you are. I mean, you're welcome to get a second opinion. But I wouldn't drive it. I mean…if it was me."

"No, no," Rosalind said distastefully. "Let's just get on with it." She grimaced noticeably.

"Let's get your information," Kate said, leading Rosalind back to the cash register.

A few moments later, Rosalind was gone, and Lizzy was scanning a long list of Prius parts on a computer screen. Kate came to her side with arms folded.

"Yes?" Lizzy asked without looking up.

"In need of love," assessed Kate. "Badly. But there's sure to be someone around here for her."

Lizzy still didn't take her eyes off the computer. "How do you know she's even gay?"

"There's no question in my mind," Kate said confidently.

Lizzy gave her lover a knowing smile. "Kate—that's what you always say."

"And have I ever been wrong?"

Lizzy stopped and looked off into mid-air. "No, actually," she said thoughtfully after a moment.

"I was right about Sally and Frankie, was I not?"

"You were right about Sally and Frankie," Lizzy confirmed. Sally and Frankie had gotten together, courtesy of the conversation corner, only six months earlier.

Her lover patted her on the shoulder. "So trust me, darling. I'm just trying to help you find customers for life."

And she was, Lizzy thought with satisfaction. Whether they knew it or not.

*

Rosalind Choi headed off in the back of her Uber in a state of vague unrest. Not only was her car now disabled and likely not to be seen for at least forty-eight hours, she felt strangely exposed.

Of course, she'd landed in a woman-owned garage, entirely peopled by lesbians. It was like stumbling onto the set of *The L Word*. Basically, she couldn't wait to get out of there.

It wasn't that Rosalind was homophobic. The issue was that Rosalind feared that she, herself, was a lesbian. It was a fact she could barely tolerate even now, in her early thirties. Even the word 'lesbian' gave her a squirrelly, uncomfortable feeling. Each time she heard it, she felt a pang of shame, as if she'd just done something terribly wrong.

Rosalind had always held out hope that she wasn't exactly a lesbian. Maybe she was just bi. She'd even dated a few men. Yet, each had been an awkward affair that never seemed to last more than a month or two. The entire subject filled her with fear and loathing.

And then there were those middle of the night longings. And the sexual dreams about women. And the fantasies. The few times she'd had sex with men, she couldn't keep her imagination at bay. When she closed her eyes, she was always making love with another woman. It was disturbing to say the least.

Hence, Rosalind had never bothered to find out the true nature of her sexuality. It was far better to stay focused on the things that really mattered in life—work, money, and success. Her own mother had long since stopped asking if there was a nice young man out there for her, and Rosalind had never bothered to set the record straight.

This was mainly because her industrious, off-the boat Chinese parents also happened to be devout Catholics. They would be mortified if they knew anything about Rosalind's longings. How many times had she been asked to get on her knees in the living room and pray to Jesus for the mortal sins of the queers? Or the *homosexuals* as her parents had chastely put it.

At such moments, she thought of the Harvard and MIT degrees, and all of the skating lessons, and ballet classes, and Girl Scout meetings, and tennis camps. Yes, there had been ample scholarships, but her parents still had to use all of their savings just to pay for the textbooks, health insurance, uniforms, plane tickets, orthodontics, and all the other endless paraphernalia of childhood.

After all they had given her, and done for her, and poured their hearts into for her, how, in a million years, could Rosalind ever tell her parents the truth?

Or tell herself, for that matter.

No, it was far better to stay strong and stay silent, and focus on work that her parents would respect, and that Rosalind could do.

Now her work was firmly in Bro World, which was a remarkably good place to hide. There, her opinion, her ideas, and her very presence seemed to barely register. Oh, they'd been insanely specific when True Wire hired her, wooing and winning her like a great trophy from LeadSpace, her former employer.

They had to have an Ivy League woman, they said. Ideally a woman of color who was fluent in Mandarin, had an MBA, an advanced engineering degree, and knew her way around legalese as well.

Rosalind had been a perfect hire with her Harvard MBA and her graduate and undergrad degrees from MIT. The Mandarin was a perk of growing up in a Chinese-American home. And as for legalese, she'd started out as a tech consultant for the Big Five law firms in Manhattan.

She'd negotiated a very beneficial deal, and now here she was. Living and working in a void in Oakland, California. She was utterly alone.

In the end, it all seemed quite anonymous and very safe. Rosalind was nothing more than a speck—a highly paid nothing on the great corporate food chain that organized True Wire. Her lesbianism was the last thing anyone there was ever going to notice, least of all her.

As the Uber sedan bumped down the pothole-strewn street, she thought once more about Driven. The Irish woman had seemed sweet enough, but why was she so insistent that Rosalind sit and talk and drink coffee? It was a garage for God's sake, not a cafe.

On the other hand, the idea of sitting for a moment and drinking coffee anywhere—even just for a half hour—did seem strangely appealing. In fact, she might still be sitting there if Kate hadn't gone on about how lesbian they all were.

That Rosalind didn't need. It just made her feel even lonelier than she already was.

The Uber pulled up in front of the gleaming new office building where True Wire's headquarters were, and Rosalind got out, happy to not think about such things any more. Setting her jaw, she headed in through the gleaming glass and chrome revolving doors.

There was work to be done.

Chapter Three

Sally opened the door of Desire's Magical Garden as a small, tinkling cluster of bells on the doorknob announced her arrival. Around her crowded shelves full of jars of herbs, crystals, potions, and elixirs displayed all manner of interesting esoterica.

A tall, commanding White woman with cascading, silver curls and pale blue eyes looked up as she entered. Her presence was neither intimidating nor gentle. Rather, she was unnervingly calm, as if she had a direct line to the gods. She gazed at Sally intently.

"Hello," the woman said. Then she studied Sally as she moved into the store.

"Hello," Sally said with a swallow. Presumably this was Desire, the store's owner, whom she'd only met on the phone so far. Calling Desire and requesting an interview had taken every ounce of courage Sally possessed.

If she hadn't been down to her last few hundred dollars, she might never have called.

Sally didn't yet have the nerve to introduce herself. Instead, she turned away and studied the display cabinet to her left, as she pretended to be a browsing customer. Glass shelf after glass shelf was covered with gold and silver rings and pendants made of various healing crystals. Some were shaped into small, pointed swords with silver handles, their hilts wrapped in sparkling cloth. Others were gleaming orbs suspended from golden chains.

Next to the vitrine, several large, dark, antique bookcases displayed row after row of tarot decks and oracle cards of every description. Two shelves held nothing but a collection of colorful crystal healing bowls and the gleaming satin cushions they rested on. Just beyond them were dozens of large, abundant looking hardcover books, many festooned with paintings and gold-embossed titles like *Golden Dawn* and *An Illustrated History of Witchcraft*.

Here and there along the shelves, a dancing Shiva statue or a Green Tara held steady in bronze. Along with them were a few well-placed sculls, eye sockets gaping. A stuffed owl with elaborately spread wings topped the book cabinet, looking over the store fiercely.

Overhead, Tibetan prayer flags and banners adorned with Celtic symbols hung from the ceiling, and a large painting of a starry night sky with horses running toward a distant horizon dominated one wall. Yet, the painting was barely noticeable behind the large, candlelit altar in front of it. Here was a tall rosewood figure of Kwan Yin, goddess of compassion, surrounded by various jars of colored candles labeled with arcane symbols.

Sally glanced down at a row of dark brown glass bottles with artisanal brown paper labels nearby. *Strong Woman Syrup*, said one. The other was apparently a tonic for *Stabilizing*. The third said simply, *Good Sex*. Nearby were several counters loaded with large and small jars of herbs, some of them green and vibrant; others, like the mugwort were more subdued and filled with small twigs.

The effect was of a wizard's curio cabinet—ageless clutter with a heavy overlay of metaphysics, astrology, and witchcraft. Yet, nothing about the store felt ominous or uncomfortable. Instead, it felt uplifting, refreshingly steady and strong. Full of ancestry and a certain, slightly dusty, magic. The smell of sage hung lightly in the air.

Finally, Sally felt empowered to approach the woman behind the counter. "Hi," she said shyly, as she drew near. The woman with the curly, silver hair scarcely looked up. "You must be Sally," she said.

Sally smiled. "Yes, I am."

"I'm Desire," she said. "Let's step into the back."

A moment later, they entered a small room, its entrance covered by a dark velvet curtain, and Sally's eyes worked to adjust to the darkness. Electric candles burned around the tiny room. A small, round table was covered with a richly patterned cloth, and a diminutive antique lamp with a silk shade cast a low, pink light around them. Desire picked up a deck of waiting cards. "Shuffle these, please." she said, handing the deck directly to Sally.

Sally took the deck, wondering what was coming next. Would she be doing the reading? Or would Desire, since she'd asked Sally to shuffle the cards. That task was usually given to the recipient. Nervously, Sally handed the now shuffled cards back to her potential employer.

Desire held the deck between her hands and closed her eyes. Her lips moved silently in some sort of prayer or invocation. Then she paused. Slowly and deliberately, Desire placed seven cards in a small spread in front of her.

Sally realized now that the deck in Desire's hands was Goddess oracle cards—the very ones she'd drawn from at home only the night before. Which was odd, given that most psychic readings were done with tarot cards. Sally smiled. She'd been worrying for days that her use of Goddess cards would be off-putting to Desire.

Not once in their phone conversation had they discussed Sally's interest or use of the Goddess oracle cards. Still, Desire had known. Apparently, Desire was good. Very good. That or she was a kindred spirit.

Desire studied the cards, then she sat back and took in Sally appraisingly. "You've got Kali in the center. Nice," she said lightly. Kali was the bringer of endings and beginnings, and a serious reminder that life usually required an ending in order to begin something new.

Sally watched, spellbound, as Desire picked her way around the circle of cards, silently putting more down and taking a few away. Yemanya, the bringer of golden opportunities, and Pele came up last. Pele always represented the pursuit of the heart's deepest desire.

Fittingly, Desire placed them in the center of the spread.

"Take one more card," Desire said to Sally encouragingly. "Find it…it's waiting for you." She displayed the deck of down-turned cards to Sally. Sally's fingertips scanned the open deck, tentatively brushing each card, waiting for the right card—the perfect card—to speak to her. It was the one, she imagined, that would seal her fate in this unexpected test of her abilities.

Momentarily, Sally's hand hesitated in mid-air. "Go on," Desire encouraged. Once more Sally's fingers scanned the deck. Still, there was no such card to be found.

Sally took a deep breath, and nearly shaking, she drew her hand back. "There isn't one," she heard herself say.

"Really?" Desire regarded her closely.

"There just…isn't," Sally said in a half-whisper.

Desire hesitated for a moment. Then she pulled all the cards off the table and began to fold them back into the deck. "Nice work," she said with a warming smile. "Pele told me you were complete as well."

Sally wasn't certain what this meant exactly. She waited in silence, but there was no further explanation. Desire rose and walked out of the readings room. Still Sally remained, unsure what to do next.

Was that…it?

Tentatively, Sally got up and found her way back into the store. Desire was working at the counter, reviewing some kind of paperwork. She glanced at Sally with a smile. "There you are," she said. "Can you start next week? I could use you three days per week."

"Yes—of course!" Sally flushed with the news. "But don't you need me to do a reading or something for you?"

"No," Desire said. "But to be clear, Sally, this is only a trial period. You'll be expected to bring in your own customers for the first several weeks you are with us, and I'll be looking in on your readings as you go. Then when the time is right, you will either be accepted on to the staff or you'll move on to the next thing."

"All right! Fine. Wonderful!" Sally gushed.

A few moments later, they shook hands and she floated toward the door, their arrangement now settled. The small cluster of bells tinkled gently behind Sally as she let herself out. She couldn't wait to tell Tenika and De—

Sally stopped, remembering with a pang of disappointment that her friends were in Belize. Well, she couldn't wait to tell Lizzy, then. And Kate.

Sally noticed she hesitated when she thought of telling her own girlfriend about her new job. Taking a deep breath, she headed up the street, feeling her belly relax. She'd done it. She'd finally landed legitimate employment, and she was proud of herself, regardless of what Frankie might think.

Now she had customers to find and appointments to book. She couldn't worry about what Frankie thought. Anyway, their fate was already written.

That much she knew for sure.

*

The therapist looked at Frankie, and tapped her pencil on her notepad contemplatively. "So what is it that makes you hold back?" she asked after a moment.

Frankie settled into the comfy confines of her therapist's Ikea armchair, and considered her question for a moment.

"Well, I mean, come on, Doc. She's beautiful, and fun, and everything. But this whole psychic business…" Frankie gave her therapist a skeptical look.

The therapist said nothing. She just sat there listening.

Frankie continued. "Look, I don't know for a fact it's bullshit, right? I mean, I'm sure Sally believes it. She's certainly not a liar or anything like that. It's just…" Helplessly, she looked at her therapist, groping for words.

Still, her therapist only listened silently.

"Help me out here, Doc," Frankie said with a smile, trying to appeal to her therapist's logical side. But that effort appeared to go nowhere. Instead, her therapist said nothing.

"Okay, so I don't believe in spirits, ghosts, visions, voices in your head, or any of that stuff, right?" Frankie continued. "I just don't. And Sally absolutely does. I mean, she's interviewing for a job as a psychic medium as we speak. And I'm either going to get with the program, or I'm screwed here."

The therapist gave a silent nod. The clock ticked on in the silence between them. Frankie glanced around the room and gave a sigh. Then she sat forward earnestly. "Look it, Doc. I want to let it all go. I want to love her unconditionally. I want to give her everything. I do," she insisted. "I just…"

Frankie's words now failed her, and she sat back defeated.

"You don't feel safe?" the therapist asked.

Frankie looked down at her hands in dismay. "Why would you say something strange like that?" she asked in a half-strangled voice.

"I'm thinking of your first date, Frankie," the therapist said. "And how unsafe you felt when she saw the source of your trauma."

"Oh…right," Frankie said slowly. "Yeah, I do remember that."

It had taken her weeks to apologize for blowing Sally off after that disastrous first date, a blind date when they played a game observing things about each other. It only took Sally a matter of moments to laser in on Tiffany, the dead child who haunted Frankie's nightmares after she found her body on Ocean

Beach. Tiffany was not only the source of Frankie's work-related PTSD, but she'd come to symbolize it as well.

After that, Frankie couldn't get out of the restaurant fast enough. That night she was convinced Sally had been set up by someone at the SFPD who wanted to get inside her head.

And yet…

Frankie could still recall the feeling that had moved through her mind when she finally ran into Sally at Driven, weeks later. Immediately, she had to apologize for blowing her off. It was as if Frankie literally had no other choice.

So, yes. There was something there, whether she cared to acknowledge it or not. It was something immeasurably huge, and still comforting and right at the same time. And it was not like any attraction Frankie had encountered before, because it stopped her cold. Which is why she was sitting here, for one hundred and fifty five dollars per hour, sorting out her most intimate thoughts with a shrink.

"But, Doc…a *psychic?*"

"Apparently," said the therapist. "There's an old saying, Frankie. First and foremost, we attract the people we most need."

"You're saying I need a woo-woo medium in my life?"

"You tell me."

Frankie shook her head. "I don't know…I don't know."

"I'm afraid that's all the time we have for today," the therapist said gently.

"If I could find tangible *proof* somehow that she was legitimate, that this whole psychic thing was for real, then maybe it would be different." Frankie paused. "I don't know. I have to think about it…"

She rose. Clearly, this inquiry was just getting started.

*

Kate folded the last of her kitchen towels in around the mixing bowls in the moving box. Glancing around the nearly empty kitchen, she did a quick calculation. What did she need for these last few days before she moved back in with Lizzy?

Coffeepot. Check. Mug. Check. Fork, knife, spoon. Cereal bowl. Plate. Scrubbee. Detergent. Check, check, check.

Even though she'd pushed to leave Lizzy's only six months earlier, now she was chomping at the bit to get back there. She'd had entirely enough of living alone in her experimental home for one. The charm of hanging her own prints and leaving the bedroom as messy as she wished had completely worn off. The fact was that she missed Lizzy terribly. It had all become unbearably lonely.

That she had to wait for the weekend, when Lizzy could once again return with her pickup and carefully reload her furniture and her belongings into the back, made her impatient.

Kate was ready to leave now.

Walking into the bedroom, she surveyed the explosion of clothing on her bed. Briefly, she'd had a misbegotten idea that she would sort through her things and give a fair amount away. But, her impatience overtook her. There was no time for that now. She wanted to spend tonight with Lizzy, and the next night, and all the nights of her life after that. She wanted to wake up beside her partner every last morning she was on Earth.

Yes. There. She'd said it. In spite of her habitual reserve, and even her fear of being so known…so vulnerable…Lizzy truly was her partner.

She wanted to listen to her steady breathing in the night. She wanted to wake up in her strong, beautifully muscled arms. Kate wanted to know that no matter where she was, or what she was doing, she had family. That someone out in the world cared about her more than anyone else.

Kate picked up a handful of t-shirts and looked around for her massive, black duffel bag on wheels. She just had to stuff it all in there, and then she would almost be done. Throw in her shoes and boots, layer in the last of her clothing, and she could just call it good.

Then Kate could get back to the business at hand—once again enjoying her rightful place in Lizzy's world.

Really, there was no longer a thing to worry about. The entire ICE thing appeared to have blown over, that much Kate knew. ICE, like all the other government agencies, was a huge bureaucracy. Kate imagined that ICE had even deactivated her file somehow, maybe because there were so many other undocumented workers to process. Therefore, it seemed like a slam dunk to move back in with Lizzy.

It seemed she could even show up at Driven once again with ease and grace. It was all part of Kate 2.0—the new more open, relaxed version of herself that was now moving through the world. ICE be damned!

Kate began throwing various pairs of heels into the duffel bag at a fast clip. If she kept up like this, she'd be done in a half hour.

Really, everything was easy. Just the mop-up that came with a major life transition.

She was ready to begin again.

Chapter Four

Frankie shifted uncomfortably in the wooden chair in the Lieutenant's office. He was on the phone in front of her, studiously ignoring her. "Yeah… Yeah. I said I would," he continued. His tone was one of complete annoyance.

It was hard for Frankie to tell if this was a business call or if he was talking to his wife, but she did her best to remain completely neutral. After all, she had a big ask to make.

Frankie glanced at her watch. She'd been sitting there for nearly ten minutes.

Finally, the Lieutenant hung up and looked at her unhappily. He had an air of exhaustion. "What do you want, Kennedy?"

She shook her head apologetically. "I'm really sorry, LT. End of the day—I know—is not a great time. I just wondered if I could get a tweak to my schedule. It's just that—"

"Now you want a change to your schedule? I thought you were up for working nights. What's it been…less than a year, Kennedy?"

"I know! I know, it's just that…"

What? Her psychic girlfriend who she couldn't talk about at work was demanding she be more available?

That wasn't even it. Sally had been nothing but accommodating, staying up until two and three in the morning to spend time with Frankie after her shift ended. That, at least, was the good part of being a psychic. You worked flexible hours.

The fact was that Frankie was craving the change herself. Once, it had been peaceful, even soothing to make the drive up 101 in the pre-dawn stillness of the middle of the night. There wasn't a soul on the road then, and those quiet night drives had managed to calm Frankie's rampant anxiety. The empty road fed her as surely as a cheeseburger in a midnight diner.

Yet now, she needed something different. Now, she wanted to live like other people—to have a pickle with that burger. Frankie wasn't sure why, but she was chalking it up to the blinking lights of the therapist's EMDR machine. Slowly but surely, she was making progress with her therapy.

Anyway, who knew? Maybe the relationship with Sally was helping to elicit change, as well. Whatever the cause, Frankie wanted to emerge back into the world of the living. She was ready to wake up with the sun once more.

"It's just that my interests have changed," Frankie now explained vaguely. "I have…you know…obligations."

Her Lieutenant raised his eyebrows. "You finally have a love life, Kennedy?"

Frankie blushed. "Well, you know…" she fumbled.

"About freaking time," the Lieutenant remarked. "But I can't just go handing out the hours just because you're in love. You don't have enough time in on the night shift. Not yet at least. But maybe soon. We'll see."

He paused now, and an electric crackle of fear suddenly moved through Frankie's body. She sensed he was about to bring up the subject no one dared talk about. Namely, her PTSD.

"So Kennedy," he began.

Frankie swallowed. "Yeah?"

"It's come to my attention that you've been doing some weird shit."

Jesus. She was right.

Frankie stalled furiously. "Like…?"

The Lieutenant's eyes bore right through her. "You know what I'm talking about."

She attempted major innocence. "Gosh, I don't…really…"

"The word is you've got trauma, Kennedy."

The Lieutenant, a former New Yorker, pronounced it 'tramma.' Clearly, he found the word distasteful. The minute an officer was outed as having PTSD—a phrase that somehow couldn't even be spoken in the station—she was marked. Like the weak link in a chain, she was now officially expected to break.

And the minute you broke, well it was sick leave as far as the eye could see. Until eventually you were forced to resign. Which made sense in a way, for they couldn't very well have damaged cops chasing down perps and waving guns around. The problem was that resignation effectively wiped out her much-needed SFPD retirement plan.

Frankie's gut took a twist. "I'm fine!" she protested. "Seriously, LT. Who's spreading this around? Because it's a bunch of bull."

Frankie still had at least eight years before she qualified for her pension. So there was no way in hell she could tell her boss what was actually going on. For that would definitely be the beginning of the end.

The Lieutenant continued to study her. "I don't know, Kennedy. I'm just saying. Watch yourself out there. If you do have *tramma* and all…" His voice trailed off.

"Don't worry. I'm fine," she repeated. Then she stood up. "Okay, that's all I guess."

"All right, then."

"Thanks, LT."

Frankie walked away as a bead of sweat trickled down her brow. She wiped at it with the back of her hand. Then putting her hands in her pockets, she felt the heft of the weapon concealed beneath her clothing.

She was okay.

She would be fine.

That's all she really had to remember.

*

Kate strolled into Driven with a bouquet of pink hothouse tulips, a tube of Lizzy's favorite chocolate lip balm and her laptop. It was time to pull up a chair in the conversation corner, and once again make herself at home.

"Wow! Twice in one week?" Lizzy leaned over and kissed Kate as she approached. "To what do I owe the pleasure?"

Kate shrugged. "I just wanted to. Here." She handed Lizzy the lip balm, and Lizzy looked up with a smile.

"Wow! Did you know I just ran out?"

Kate shrugged mysteriously and headed off to the corner. "I have to put these in water," she said.

"Glad you're here, baby. And nice flowers!" Lizzy called after her. Then she returned to the engine in front of her. Kate glanced back to meet her eyes and they both smiled.

It felt incredibly right to be at the garage, Kate thought to herself as she reached under the sink for a vase and began to fill it up. A woman sat in the conversation corner. She was an older woman with blue eyes, a rounded face, and a ready grin. She was working on a jigsaw puzzle at the table.

"Hey," she said as Kate approached.

"Can I get you a coffee?" Kate asked.

"Seriously? Of course!" The woman smiled up at her, her eyes crinkling in well-worn happy wrinkles. "I heard this was the place to be. And if you have some cream, then I'll seriously be impressed."

"Oh, we do indeed," said Kate, snapping a pod into the coffee maker and setting up a cup for one.

"I'm Kate, by the way," she said, introducing herself to the blue-eyed woman.

"Alice," she said, and they shook hands. "You look familiar to me…"

"I'm Lizzy's partner," Kate explained.

Partner. There. She said it. Out loud and to a stranger, even. For this was indeed the official state of things. Kate smiled to herself, and wondered if Lizzy had heard her. It felt real, and it felt good.

Alice raised her eyebrows and nodded approvingly. "Nice," she said. "Wait—you're a friend of Sally's, right?"

Kate smiled. "You know our Sally?"

"I do! I even have a small pile of her business cards in my pocket. She just called me, actually. A shop on Grand hired her to do readings, but we've got to help her book some. I thought we could leave a few around here." Alice handed a small stack of Sally's cards over to Kate.

Wordlessly, Kate studied them. Then leaning in, Alice lowered her voice. "Just retired from my job in Big Pharma sales, so you can bet I'm getting a reading, pronto." She hesitated. "If you girls know anyone who likes older women, I'm beyond available."

Kate gave her an easy grin. "Good luck—" she managed to say, but she was cut off by the sudden arrival of Rosalind, clearly here to pick up her car.

"Rosalind—lovely to see you!"

"Hi there," Rosalind said, a little breathlessly.

"I'm sure Lizzy's almost ready for you." Kate motioned to the woman at the table. "This is Alice. Why don't you have a seat, and I'll go see how long it will be."

Rosalind nodded and, pulling out a chair, sat down tentatively. Immediately, Alice began to chat her up in earnest. Kate smiled as she walked away. Alice and Rosalind seemed like an unlikely pair, but you never knew.

A moment later Kate was back. "Lizzy's still hard at it, so I'm afraid she's going to need a bit more time if you can wait.

We're almost there. Coffee?" she asked, but then she noticed that Rosalind had already helped herself at the machine.

Meanwhile, Rosalind leaned back in her chair and folded her arms across her chest. "Okay. Thanks." She glanced at her watch and sighed. She looked none too pleased.

"You must have a high-pressure job, huh?" Alice asked, sliding the final piece into one of the puzzle's edges.

Rosalind shrugged. "I don't know… I suppose. I haven't worked there very long."

Alice looked at her curiously. "Oh?"

Rosalind shrugged. "I'm in online security."

"Ah." Alice was quiet for a moment. "A man's world."

Now Kate cut in. "You're new to Oakland, aren't you, Rosalind? I thought you told me that…"

"Yeah, I'm new," Rosalind said. She cleared her throat a little awkwardly, then she stood up. "I should really go—" she began, but Kate cut her off.

"Now, now, love, Lizzy really is almost done. She promised it would be no more than a few minutes. Why don't you work on the puzzle? Or perhaps you have your own things to attend to."

"You can put the sky together," Alice offered, pushing a pile of blue edge pieces in Rosalind's direction. "That will keep you busy."

Rosalind regarded them both dubiously for a moment, but then she suddenly began studying the pieces. "I haven't done a puzzle in years," she said.

"Yeah, I haven't either," said Alice. "I think that part of my brain still works. Maybe."

Rosalind's gaze was held fast by the puzzle pieces as she spread them out before her. Kate sat down on the couch to watch as Rosalind's head bent further over in concentration, her shiny black hair spilling across the table.

Slowly, she began to assemble a few pieces. Then a few more. Rosalind's hand moved faster and faster as more and more of the pieces seemed to magically snap into place. Meanwhile, Alice looked on in mild wonder.

After several more moments, Rosalind looked up, slightly flushed. Half of the sky was now neatly in place.

"Damn," Alice said. "Are you sure you're not a pro?"

"There are professional puzzle people?"

"Probably," Alice bluffed. "There are professional everything else, so why not?"

Rosalind shrugged. "I'm good with spatial dynamics." She glanced over at Kate. "Any progress?"

Kate stood up. "Let me check."

"So you're new in town?" Alice asked. "I mean…I don't even know why I'm suggesting this, but maybe you should get a reading with my friend Sally. She's a psychic, like a tarot reader. Well, actually she reads Goddess cards. But she's really good, and—"

Rosalind stood up and glanced around, effectively cutting Alice off. Then she looked down at her awkwardly. "I don't believe in psychics," she explained. "I'm a hard science person. So I'm all set." She paused and looked at Alice. "Thanks, anyway. For sharing the puzzle, I mean."

"Yeah, I know this seems like a crazy thing. But here." Now Alice was pushing one of Sally's cards on Rosalind. "You might find it useful somehow. Just take it for a rainy day, right?"

"Okay. Fine." Rosalind took the card and gamely shoved it into her pocket. But her eyes were already moving elsewhere, as she glanced around for the location of her car. "Do I see Lizzy finishing?" she asked Kate.

Lizzy was now closing the hood of the car and peeling off her lavender latex gloves. She motioned Rosalind over to her, and Rosalind picked up her bag and marched off briskly in the direction of her car.

Alice looked over at Kate and shrugged. "I tried," she said, and Kate nodded with a smile.

"Nice work," she said sympathetically. Both of them watched as Rosalind stepped up to the cash register and paid for her repair.

"Techies," said Alice with a sigh.

Kate just smiled.

*

Rosalind drummed her fingertips on the edge of the steering wheel as she waited for the light to change. Yet again, she'd been completely unnerved by her visit to Driven.

What was with that place, anyway?

Yes, okay, they did the repair relatively fast, and the car appeared to be fine. The price was even right. But what was up with the pushy woman with the business cards? And why on earth did these people even care who she was, or what she did?

For a moment, Rosalind contemplated the fact that Alice might be hitting on her. The thought actually made her laugh out loud. Obviously, that was not going to happen, but why did it even matter? And why was she so bugged?

Just because it was all so free and easy? And lesbian?

The light changed, and Rosalind stepped hard on the accelerator, feeling her car silently speed ahead. It was as if Driven had somehow found its way under her skin and straight into her veins. It was an uncomfortable, too close feeling. This was intimacy she just didn't want.

Digging the spurned business card out of her pocket, she tossed it into the backseat, determined to get it away from her. Then shaking her head, Rosalind decided she was done with the place. Next time, she was heading for some Bro garage. Just like right now she was heading for her Bro job in the Bro tech firm.

The dudes might be crude, sexist, entitled, rude, and arrogant. But at least they didn't presume to even know her…or want to know her. Instead, she could be blissfully alone.

That was just how she liked it.

*

Sally and Frankie got out of Frankie's truck and surveyed the beach spread out before them. It was a glorious day—a Tuesday. Frankie's day off.

Here was the end of the world, or at least that's what it felt like. The rugged Sonoma coast, spreading off to the north and south. Its dark, jagged rocks and crumbling, red cliffs met the pulsing white lace of the surf for as far as the eye could see. Sea stacks of wet, black rocks and rock arches stood out starkly in the splashing waves.

Frankie and Sally smiled at each other, and for a moment they held hands as they stood there beholding the sea.

There was something crashing and spectacular about the Pacific; it was big, loud, and dramatic in every way. Down below the cliff they stood on, Californians were dwarfed by the magnitude of the sea. Their small figures ran and walked along a white sand beach dotted with big, gray logs of driftwood. Dogs cavorted at the edge of the surf, and wild-looking, suntanned children in outgrown wetsuits came peeling out of the waves on their boogie boards.

"Let's go," Sally said, tugging Frankie's hand toward the beach.

"Wait, we can't leave anything in the truck."

Sally looked down at the picnic and the blanket in her arms. "What are we leaving?"

Walking back to the truck, Frankie pulled her small, ever-present backpack out from behind the driver's seat. It was her Go Bag, and she always had it on her in case of an earthquake or a wildfire. It was nothing much, she insisted. Just emergency supplies. A few boxes of water. Ready-to-eat military meals, and a heating source. First aid supplies. A compass, a few maps. Dust masks. Space blankets. Emergency radio and batteries.

And as ever, her weapon.

Sally sighed. By now she should be used to this. "Really?"

"Sorry, honey. You know I have to."

"But—" Sally began. It wasn't the emergency supplies that threw her every time, it was the fact that wherever her girlfriend went, a gun went, too, along with several rounds of ammo. She knew she just had to get used to it.

Sally turned away and began scrambling down the cliff. "Whatever," she said dismissively over her shoulder. Frankie now clamored after her, struggling to get a firm foothold on the crumbling soil beneath her boots.

"Anyway, you can't leave stuff in your vehicle at beaches," Frankie called after Sally. "They're hit on four times as much as other places. A beach is break-in central."

Sally turned to her. "It's your day off, Sergeant."

Frankie grimaced. "Right. Okay…okay. Never mind."

They hiked down on to the beach in silence for another moment. "Oh!" Frankie said. "I almost forgot. I asked the Lieutenant about changing my hours, so I could be on the day shift."

Sally turned and looked at Frankie with a smile. "Really? You did that?"

"Yeah. I mean, he's not going to let me change. Yet. But the thing with the Lieutenant, you see, is you have to get the idea rolling around in the back of his head."

"Or the top of his mind," said Sally lightly.

Frankie stopped. "What?"

"Nothing. It's just that he might surprise you sooner rather than later. That's all."

Frankie shook her head. "Now, come on, baby. You know I'm not into the prognosticating and all that…"

"Do you see my deck of cards? Are we having a reading? No, you don't. Because it's just a gut feeling, Frankie. That's all it is, so take it or leave it."

"Fair enough," Frankie said. Then she reached for Sally's hand. "Anyway," she said. "I'm trying."

"You are indeed," noted Sally. She smiled at her girlfriend. "And here we are in one of the most beautiful places on Earth."

Frankie put down her pack and looked around. "Yup."

It was at moments like this when Frankie felt a new and un-accustomed rightness in her time with Sally. As they stood there on the beach, her shoulders relaxed, her jaw softened, and for just a moment, she forgot all of it. The pressure of her job. The anxiety that poured through her body non-stop. The unforgettable, lifeless image of Tiffany, the dead girl back at Ocean Beach who was ironed into her memory.

Instead, for once Frankie felt perfectly at ease. She could walk for twenty miles on this coast with Sally, as long as they walked together. She'd go anywhere Sally wanted her to go, and do anything she wanted. It was comfort her soul badly needed.

Frankie spread out the blanket on the beach, and then, sitting down, she patted the space beside her. "Come here," she said, and Sally sat down. Frankie's arm came around her. Then slowly, in a perfect, innocent moment of surrender, Sally's head dropped to her shoulder.

There they sat for the longest time. Enveloped in a perfect peace amidst the crashing waves.

Chapter Five

Lizzy popped a handful of pumpkin seeds into her mouth and crunched. She still had a tire rotation and a pair of brake rotors to replace, and it was nearly five. Today had been just a little too long. Lizzy sighed, squared her shoulders, and studied the minivan slowly rising before her on the lift.

She had no idea running the garage alone was going to be this intense. Tenika couldn't get back here fast enough.

Wiping her hands on her coveralls, Lizzy took another look at her worksheet. Judging from the minivan's aging paint job, Lizzy was just about certain that the bolts would be rusted, if not corroded.

Tucking the new rotors under her arm, she picked up a can of lubricant spray from her workbench. Thoughtfully, Lizzy surveyed the spent brakes that were now overhead. She scratched her chin and sighed. It was just as she thought. The whole damn thing was a mess.

A few moments later, Lizzy was wrestling with some especially rusty caliper fasteners when she heard footsteps behind her. "Hello?" a male voice said.

Instinctively, a shot of adrenaline zapped her spine, and Lizzy turned around. Three burly men dressed in black walked toward her in the gathering afternoon gloom of the garage. One of them, a tall, blond man with a regulation crew cut, wore a navy bulletproof vest that said POLICE—ICE in large, white letters. A police badge was affixed to his vest, as were a set of keys, and a black walkie-talkie.

His expression was neither friendly nor menacing. Instead, he was a study in calm, professional neutrality. A weapon was placed securely at his side, as were a pair of handcuffs. The cuffs rattled against his leg as he walked.

The officer was carrying a piece of paper in his hand. "Katherine Morahan?" he asked in a loud monotone. The three men stopped just short of where Lizzy was working under the lift. Immediately, Lizzy noticed the forearm of one of the agents. The word 'Brooklyn' was tattooed across his biceps in large block letters.

Lizzy ignored the intense fear that was now pouring through her body. Instead, she faced them and folded her arms.

Her internal chant began in earnest. *Be cool. Be cool. Be cool.* "No…I'm not Katherine Morahan," she told them. "I'm Lizzy Edgewood. I'm one of the owners."

The officer was nonplussed. "ID, please, ma'am."

Immediately, Lizzy turned toward her backpack on the counter, but the agent suddenly stopped her. "Wait," he said. His hand did not leave her arm. Instead, he tightened his grip and glanced around behind him "Where is your ID?" the officer asked.

"It's in my backpack. Over there." Lizzy nodded with her head. "My ID is in my wallet in the front pocket." One of the two men now dutifully went over, opened Lizzy's backpack, dug around for a moment, and then produced her wallet. He rifled through it until he found her California driver's license.

He inspected it. Then walking back, he handed it to the officer in charge with a nod. "We have reason to believe Ms. Morahan works in this garage," the officer continued.

"Well, she doesn't. It's just me and my business partner, Tenika Cummins, and Tenika's in Belize on vacation. So basically it's just me right now." Lizzy nodded to the brake job on the lift behind her. "If I could get back to my work—"

"Yeah," the officer interrupted. "That's not going to happen."

The first man now nodded to the other two who spread out immediately, and began methodically looking through every part of the garage. Lizzy watched one of them open the door to the storage area and bathroom, and disappear inside. Another one was busy rifling through the papers on her desk.

"Uh, excuse me," she said to the man in charge. "I think you need a search warrant to go through my place."

The commanding officer just chuckled and ignored her.

Lizzy took a deep breath and steadied herself once more. The commanding officer began opening and closing some of the doors of the cars waiting to be repaired.

"Yeah…I…" Truthfully, Lizzy had no idea what the legalities were around having her own property searched. She decided to stop talking. Instead, she watched the men move around the garage with a sinking feeling.

ICE had arrived. In her garage. This was actually happening. She thanked God Kate wasn't there at the moment.

Now Lizzy tried to remember the legal documents she'd read about ICE raids months earlier.

Her mind spun in circles. There was something about the warrant…it needed to be signed by someone? A judge perhaps?

"Uh…officer—" she began, but the lead ICE agent was not listening. Instead he was speaking into his radio and steadfastly ignoring her. "Uh…sir?" she began again.

Now he turned away from her and went to discuss things with the officer going through the manifest. A surge of fear hit Lizzy, and she tried to think clearly. She had contacted Kate on that computer, but only once, around the flat tire repair that originally brought Kate into the garage. All of their other communication had been via text or phone.

Still, it was probably only a matter of moments until they demanded Lizzy surrender her phone. She cleared her throat, meaning to speak. But then she glanced at the piece of paper the officer in front of her held in his hand.

It was a warrant for Kate's arrest, complete with photograph. Lizzy could see Kate's name neatly typed at the top. A slow, nauseous feeling began to overtake her, but still she held steady.

"I mean…I'm sorry, officer. I'd love to help you, but I can't," Lizzy said to his back. "I don't even remember the last time I saw her. I'm afraid I have no idea where she is."

Now the ICE officer whirled around and got right in her face. "Making false statements to a peace officer in the state of California will get you up to six months in jail, and a thousand dollar fine, ma'am."

Momentarily, Lizzy was slightly stunned. Then quickly she recouped. *Keep it friendly*, she cautioned herself. *Polite and professional.*

"I'm sure that's true, Officer, but actually I'm not lying," Lizzy continued evenly. She tried to strike a conciliatory tone. "Please feel free to search the place. Look around all you want. I mean… I'm happy to help you if you just tell me what you need."

The officer didn't move. His piercing blue eyes seemed to be taking her apart, piece by piece, and Lizzy swallowed hard. She felt herself start to weaken slightly under his gaze. But then she planted her feet a little more firmly and took another breath.

They continued to stare at each other. "Are you aware that Katherine Morahan is an undocumented alien?" the officer asked. "Our records show she worked in your garage."

Lizzy shook her head. "I barely know Katherine," she bluffed. "Anyway, no… I had no idea. We never discussed it."

He pulled back slightly now, surveying her up and down with a long, appraising look. Then shaking his head, he sighed. "Stand down," he said to the other two, and both of them immediately looked up. A little reluctantly, the two officers stopped what they were doing and moved toward the door.

The officer followed. But then glancing over his shoulder, he glared at Lizzy once more. "We'll be back if it turns out you're lying."

Suddenly, the garage was empty. Lizzy was as alone as she had been only moments earlier.

Fuck.

Grabbing her cell phone with a shaking hand, she called Kate. The phone rang once, then twice.

Her heartbeat was racing now as Lizzy silently pleaded for Kate to respond. *Pick up. Pick up. Pick up.*

Kate answered on the third ring.

"Honey?" Lizzy began. "We're screwed."

*

Kate clicked off her cell phone and looked around her apartment frantically.

Under the bed. Yes, under the bed would work.

Getting on her hands and knees, she found a place for herself amidst the dust kitties and the old tissues. Kate curled up in fetal position on the dirty wooden floor and waited, her phone still in her trembling hands.

Her heart was on fire, beating wildly. Every creak she heard, every footfall sounded like ICE was already pounding at the door, ready to arrest her. Kate closed her eyes and waited. She thanked God she'd gotten groceries to last a few days, and that her car was full of gas.

Lizzy said they could be coming for her at any moment. That she couldn't open the door under any circumstances, no matter how loud or threatening they were. Nor should Kate indicate in any way that she was even home. In fact, Lizzy told her to stay out of view and keep the lights off.

Kate had never heard her lover sound like this before. Lizzy's voice was shaking, and her usual strong woman demeanor was nowhere to be seen. ICE apparently knew far more about Kate then either she or Lizzy had assumed. It appeared they'd been doing all kinds of research on her and her whereabouts.

Kate's spinning mind now turned to more practical matters. Much as Lizzy had emphasized she should stay out of sight, she realized she couldn't stay under the bed all night. At some point, she was going to have to get up off of this hard, dirty floor and actually finish packing her things. For that was the other thing.

Lizzy was now madly searching for a sanctuary church that would take Kate in as a resident until her legal status was resolved. Lizzy was even creating a Go Bag for Kate, with emergency supplies and food, which she'd be delivering at two o'clock tomorrow morning, when they made their move. Assuming Lizzy could find a church that would even house Kate.

In the meanwhile, well…here she was. Hiding under her bed.

Kate wiggled her way out and sat up on the bedroom floor. She ran a worried hand through her hair. Clearly this was a bit of overreaction. Larger questions, however, still loomed.

What the hell was she going to do now?

Kate stood up and walked into the kitchen, where she turned on the electric kettle. She would begin with a nice strong cup of tea. That seemed to help everything at times like this.

For now at least, she'd also stay away from the windows and keep the lights off.

And, of course, she'd fret.

*

Rosalind leaned back in her chair and stretched overhead. Her body had that stuck-to-the-chair feeling that came with too many hours of staring at her screen, reading AI research.

She was ready to think about something else entirely. Standing up, Rosalind considered her options. Graze at the office's Endless Snack Bar, which was mostly a junk candy stand filled with Twizzlers and Skittles, plus a waffle maker. Grab a brew at the Drink & Think Station, just past the men's room, which was the agency's thinly disguised bar (though, yes, they did offer kombucha in addition to a host of craft brews.) Or perhaps she'd go jump on the air-string trampoline in what used to be the conference room.

As usual, none of them appealed. But then, what did she expect from the place? A meditation room with a fake waterfall? Rosalind headed for her old reliable: the ladies' room. To get there, she had to descend two floors.

Moments later, Rosalind swung open the door and headed for a stall. She locked herself in and sat down to pee. As she did, she contemplated her day so far. Achievable goals met: zero. Friendly water cooler chats: also zero. Bosses, assistants, or anyone looking in on her for even a few seconds: zero. Brilliant strokes of genius: zero.

Any kind of instructions on what she should be doing in her so-called job: zero as well.

Single-spaced pages of university studies on things like support-vector machines, stochastic gradient descent, gradient boosting, bounded decision trees, and random forests consumed: close to 100. Rosalind was not doing this because she'd been asked to. So far, she'd been asked to do nothing but "*observe*" in her boss's words.

So basically, Rosalind was observing her little heart out, digging around and trying to learn as much about this company as she could. Currently, she was studying the systems they were testing for the next generation of AI Fake News detection.

And she was doing what she always did. Specifically, she was looking for holes.

It was day sixteen at Rosalind's new job, and she seriously wondered when some kind of actual assigned work might begin. She'd considered speaking to her boss, but both times she stopped herself. Somehow, it felt right to stay silent and just keep watching.

From the safety of her locked stall, Rosalind heard the bathroom door swing open. Then two women entered and stopped at the sink. She didn't recognize their voices.

"Oh, she seems benign enough," one said.

"Yeah, well, probably because no one wants to sleep with her," the other replied. "I just can't figure out whose side she's on. I mean…there are, like, zero indicators."

"I'm telling you, she's just another vanilla good girl. Mom and Dad were apparently Christian missionaries or something."

"Wait—she grew up here?"

"Well, yeah. You know, Chinese evangelicals. Whatever."

Rosalind's face suddenly turned hot, and now she longed to see who these women were. They had to be talking about her. How did these two know her background—and who the hell were they?

Silently, she picked up her feet and rested them on the edge of the toilet seat, so neither her pants nor her shoes could be seen or identified.

"Well, you don't know for sure she's such a goody-goody…" one woman posited.

"Oh, I do. I got hold of her interview file and the background check. She's practically a Catholic saint, so presumably she'll be excellent at doing what she's told."

"Well, that or she'll start a revolt."

"Wait 'til Berring fills her in. She'll probably be gone in a heartbeat."

The two women were talking about Scott Berring, Rosalind's frat boy boss, known for his Maserati collection, which he enjoyed racing around the curves of Skyline Boulevard at night. Rosalind swallowed and tried to fight the fear that was rising in her belly.

The first woman lowered her voice to a near whisper and now Rosalind strained to hear what was being said. She could only make out a few words.

"…keep her neutral…"

The second woman gave a bitter laugh. "Sounds fucking impossible."

Then the door swung open once again, and they left.

Until that moment, she'd assumed she was the only woman in the entire place. And that barely anyone even knew she was there.

*

"May I have Father Dunleavy?" Lizzy asked. She glanced at her watch. It was nearing eight o'clock, an hour when no self-respecting priest or rabbi would still be kicking around their place of worship. She couldn't imagine who was still answering the phone in any of these places.

Lizzy was put on hold, and she glanced over the remaining names of official sanctuary centers on her list. All that was left was a mosque, a Unitarian church, and a Hispanic church.

The person who answered the phone now returned. "Father Dunleavy is gone for the day," he said.

Lizzy cleared her throat and began hopefully. "Okay, well, I'm actually calling to see if you have any space for someone seeking sanctuary."

"Oh, no, I'm afraid we're more than full," the man told her. *More than full.* Lizzy's mind went to people sleeping in the pews. "But best of luck to you. Feel free to come by and worship," he added.

Lizzy mumbled her thanks and hung up, trying to avoid the despair that was rising through in her throat like a dark cloud of doom. She took a deep breath and considered the list again. The mosque was next on her list.

Now Lizzy paused. She looked back at the list again. The Unitarian church stopped her. Momentarily, she closed her eyes and concentrated. The name of the place seemed strangely familiar. But why?

What was her connection to the place?

In an instant, the face of a diffident, gender-queer musician who played piano at a Unitarian church in Oakland came to mind. Lizzy had met them at the garage. Could it be possible this was their –church—Unitarian Universalists for Peace and Justice?

And if so, what was their name? Could Lizzy even find this person? Because if there was anything she needed right now, it was an inside connection.

There were three other Unitarian churches in the Bay Area, and Lizzy had already called all of them. Each one had told her they were either full or they didn't actually take sanctuary seekers.

Lizzy squeezed her eyes shut in concentration. She had to remember this person's name. She simply had to. It was that or leave Kate to hide out for the rest of her days in an apartment ICE may or may not know about.

For a moment, Lizzy considered heading back to the garage and going through all the customer records they kept on file. There were hundreds of repair orders, so how was she going to even know which one it was? She couldn't remember what the repair had been, let alone the first name of one of their customers.

There really was only one answer, of course. She was going to have to call Tenika.

Chapter Six

"Wait...just hold that thought in your mind while I shuffle the deck." Sally put her phone down and shuffled the Goddess cards on the kitchen table in front of her. Then she picked up the phone again. "Are you still thinking about it?"

Kate's voice was painted with pain. "Sally, love, what else am I going to think about right now?"

"Good point." Sally laid out a five-card sequence. She studied the cards for only a moment. "Ohhhh...you've got this, Kate. You seriously do."

"Say more, please."

"I don't see any reason to be alarmed. I mean, I know these are big, scary, police guys and everything. But actually, it's kind of funny. Cordelia is in the first position, which is the immediate past, and she's urging you to go outside. You've been cooped up for too long."

Kate was dumbfounded. "Seriously?"

"That's what the cards say, at least. As for what's happening right now, Guinevere is reversed. So, there is some kind of trouble in the department of True Love."

Kate sighed. "Yes. I suppose there is, given that I was just about to move in with Lizzy. And now, well, I'll be lucky to find a church to live in."

Sally continued, a little breathlessly. "But—Kate—this card can be so much bigger than just romantic love. It could be about your relationship with yourself. Perhaps you feel some guilt or shame about the situation. Or you long to get on the evolutionary fast track with this experience."

Kate swallowed. "Really, love, top of my mind is whether I'll be arrested."

"Yeah, well, I don't see that happening," Sally continued. "This is all about karma and learning—that's all any of this is, right? I mean, in the last position is Kwan Yin, reversed. So something is up with your natural compassion. Are you being really judgmental of anyone right now?"

"I'm not particularly thrilled with ICE, I have to say."

As she said this, Kate couldn't help thinking of Frankie. Certainly, Frankie had nothing to do with her attempted arrest. Frankie had already shown up as a true supporter of Driven. Kate would never forget how she had helped them get a restraining order against her former boss who was threatening both Kate and Lizzy.

Still, a cop was a cop. Or so she imagined.

"I suppose the ICE people are just doing their jobs..." Kate murmured, doing her best to sound compassionate. Her voice trailed off as her mind flashed, yet again, to getting on a plane back to Ireland.

There was tear-stained Lizzy's face at the airport. And the grim reality of entering her parents' threadbare living room with the 1978 shag carpet and the sad, faded pictures of sunsets and sailboats on the walls. And the almost certain job she would have, once again, of pulling pints at the family pub for a crew of fat, elderly drunken men. Just as she had when she was barely a teenager.

This would become her world once more, for she'd have to stay there, at least initially. It was that or...Kate didn't know what. Really, she couldn't even think that far out. If only she had more money, or a lawyer. Or anything that would help her get out of this.

Kate sighed. "Guess I'd better work on my compassion."

"Yeah, well, I wouldn't worry," Sally concluded. "The Goddesses say you're going to be okay. Really. You'll be fine, Kate."

The news settled in like a subtle rain—damp and somewhat chilly. But then, what was she expecting? Nothing Sally could tell her would soothe her completely rattled nerves now.

Sally cut into her thoughts. "Oh…that's interesting. I pulled another card about the arc of your situation. It's Artemis, the Guardian. I'm telling you Kate…you really have got this. Artemis tells us that our loved ones are safe, and we are safe, as long as we're all together."

Now Kate's voice spiraled up in a shrill tirade of frustration. "Yes, I'm sure, that's the exact problem, Sally! We can't actually be together. And here, I've finally said 'yes' to Lizzy. I'm finally ready for her…" She paused, attempting to get hold of herself as tears of frustration filled her eyes.

Kate took a deep breath. "I'm sorry," she backtracked. "No need to take it out on you, love. I know you're just trying to help me."

Sally made soothing sounds on the other end of the phone. "The Universe, the Angels, and all your other guides have your back, Kate. They truly do." Now Sally paused once more. "You and Lizzy will be together again. Maybe it won't be immediately, but it will be in good time. I'm sure of it."

Kate took this in with a sigh. "Okay," she said simply. Perhaps this was somehow the truth, though her mind could scarcely grasp it.

She would have to just wait and see.

*

Frankie was waiting in the checkout line, cradling a New York strip steak, a pint of chocolate ice cream, and a pound of Yukon Gold potatoes with one arm, and a six pack of lager with the other. She couldn't get home fast enough after another long, wearying day.

A woman joined her in the line and Frankie glanced over her shoulder at her. At this hour, well past midnight, there weren't usually too many people in the twenty-four-hour Safeway. Usually, it was just her and a few drag queens looking for snacks after a long night. *The Gafeway* they called it, given that it was in the Castro.

But now, improbably, a small crowd was gathering. The elderly man ahead of her (why was he even awake?) was having trouble deciding which lottery card to pick. Frankie sighed, shifted her load, and glanced around hopefully for another open cash register. There wasn't one.

There never was at this hour.

There was a tap on her arm. "Excuse me." It was the woman behind her. Frankie glanced over her shoulder at her. She appeared to be middle aged, well dressed with silver hair and a professorial look. The woman shoved her glasses up the bridge of her nose and peered at Frankie.

Meanwhile, the elderly man was now scrutinizing his super scratcher card and shaking his head dubiously. The ice cream Frankie was holding had rendered her arm numb. Frankie leaned forward in her best help-the-public mode. "Sir, may I assist you?"

The elderly man turned around in slow motion and looked at her blankly. Meanwhile, the woman behind her tapped on her shoulder more insistently. "Miss?" Frankie heard her say.

Her fingers lingered on Frankie's arm, and she shook the woman's touch off of her as she exchanged looks with the cashier. "Sir, you need to decide," the cashier said.

"May I help?" Frankie asserted hopefully. Then suddenly the woman behind her was right in her ear.

"I can see your aura, and you are in terrible pain," the woman said. "It's all red."

Frankie spun around and looked at the woman, who now looked quite disheveled. Perhaps she was drunk. Or psychotic. Frankie regarded her more closely. "I'm sorry?"

The woman nodded to the space above Frankie's head. "It's actually a little purple up there. But don't worry. All you have to do is eat some valerian root. That's what I do." She smiled pleasantly at Frankie. Then her voice dropped to a conspiratorial whisper. "They have it at Whole Foods."

Frankie sighed. *Damn, it had been a long day.* She turned back to the man in front of her. He looked up at her with tears in his eyes. "I just wanted the one with the horses on it," he said.

"The super scratcher's good," Frankie said. But the man shook his head woefully.

Now the cashier took charge. "Mister, we haven't got any cards with any horses. You want the super scratcher; get the super scratcher. People are waiting."

The old man's agitation ratcheted up now. "Wait! I can't get that one—I know I can't! They told me to get the one with the horses."

"Sir—" Frankie began, but once again the woman behind her chimed in.

"Walnuts, too," she said. "Excellent when you're all red."

Jesus Christ. Frankie had had enough.

She slammed her steak, her ice cream, her potatoes, and her beer on the conveyor belt. "Would you just freaking make a decision?" she demanded of the old man. He looked at her in horror, and now tears began to stream down his face. He stared at his trembling hands, dumbfounded.

Instantly, Frankie regretted her outburst. She patted the old man on the back. "I'm sorry, sir, I just think you need some assistance."

"They told me to get the ones with the horses," he kept murmuring. "If they don't have horses, I can't get them." His crying overtook him now.

Reaching inside her shirt, Frankie fished out the badge that hung around her neck and flashed it at the cashier. "I'll call nine-one-one," she said. "I'll handle him. Just put my stuff on the side."

This was her life, she thought grimly as she helped the man out of the grocery line. There was always some crazy person somewhere, demanding to be helped. In San Francisco they were ubiquitous, and they managed to find her like she was some freaking magnet. Especially when she was off duty. Tonight, she was actually surrounded by them.

Frankie escorted the bewildered, elderly man over to a corner by the front door while they waited for the police. "They told me the horses were the winners," he tried to explain.

"Who told you?"

"Them." The old man looked vacantly around. He waved his hand through the air. "You know?"

Frankie rolled her eyes. This was exactly why she couldn't totally relax around Sally. Because Sally believed in 'Them,' too. If Frankie hadn't spent so much time moving crazy people around in her professional life, maybe it would be different.

"Someone's coming who can help you figure it out right now, sir."

"Will they know about the cards with the horses?" he asked hopefully.

A little while later, a patrol car with flashing lights pulled up outside the store, and two uniformed officers walked in and looked around. A moment later they were escorting the confused man back to his home, and Frankie was paying for her half-melted ice cream and her steak.

She hauled her paper bag of groceries out to her car, happy to finally be on her way home. As she climbed into the driver's seat, the phone rang. Frankie pulled out her phone, curious to see who was calling her at this hour.

It was Lizzy, calling her at nearly two a.m. Frankie answered immediately. "Lizzy? Everything okay?"

Lizzy's voice sounded supremely tired. "Hey." She sighed audibly. "Frankie, I don't know if this is a good time, but Sally said this is when you get off work—"

"No, no it's fine. What's up?"

A moment later Frankie hung up and started her engine. Really, the world was full of shit sometimes. At least, that's all she could make of it. She wouldn't let Lizzy talk much about it on the phone, but she already had an idea what was happening. ICE was after Kate, and she needed to help however she could.

Tomorrow, she'd learn more while she took a walk with Lizzy. She pulled up to a stoplight and waited patiently, even though Market Street was now completely deserted. Why ICE would deport someone like Kate, who'd done basically nothing, was beyond her. It wasn't like she had any sort of criminal record. Or anything, really.

The world had gotten mighty strange.

That much Frankie knew for sure.

*

"Is that really you? Thank God!" Lizzy began.

Tenika's voice was scratchy with static over the landline. "You okay? The garage burn down or something?"

"I'm fine, Driven is fine. Everything's fine… How's the snorkeling?"

"It's great. Lizzy, why the hell are you calling me?"

"It's Kate. I'm worried about her."

Tenika gave a heavy sigh. "Seriously? You're calling me about Kate? Here?" Tenika had witnessed a lot of Lizzy's romantic dramas over the years.

"No—hear me out, T. ICE came by the garage. They're on to her, Tenika. I think they even may know where she lives. We've got to get her into some kind of sanctuary church like…yesterday."

Tenika's voice spiraled up in alarm. "*Jesus*. Are you shitting me?"

"I wish I was. I thought you knew someone—a gender-queer person who we took care of…you remember them? Mendle…or Milo. I can't remember their name, but I know she worked for the Unitarians?"

"Monroe. We fixed their timing belt. And she's not a she—she's a 'they.' Don't screw that up."

"Monroe! Right!" Immediately, Monroe's face came flooding back into Lizzy's memory. "Thank God for your memory! You don't remember their last name, do you?"

"Nope, but I remember the church. That Peace and Justice place..." she began vaguely.

"The Unitarian Center for Peace and Justice?"

"That's it. Give Monroe a call. They'll help you out."

"Amazing! Thank you...thank you so much!"

"Okay, I gotta get off the phone. The fishing boat is waiting for me."

Lizzy chucked. Of course it was. "Go catch the big one," she said. "And T—seriously. Thank you."

Lizzy hung up and took her first full breath all day. She had hoped to move Kate the night before, but she had yet to find a church that would take her in. Now hope had reared its head once more.

May Monroe be the answer to all of their problems.

Chapter Seven

First the pounding happened in Kate's dream. A sledgehammer was coming down again and again, destroying the hood of her car. She couldn't see who was using it, but the destruction was total.

Suddenly, Kate sat bolt upright in bed as a shot of fear raced through her body.

The pounding was real, and it was coming from the building entrance down at the street. Now her buzzer rang, long and loud. A garbled male voice yelled through the intercom downstairs. "Katherine Morahan. Open the door."

Shit. This almost certainly was ICE.

They'd found her.

Terrified, Kate looked around, uncertain where to go or even what to do. The clock next to her blinked as it reported the time: 5:03a.m. She picked up her phone from the bedside table and began frantically punching in Lizzy's number as the pounding on the street continued.

There were a few more lengthy jabs on the buzzer. "OPEN UP!" the voice insisted.

Meanwhile, Lizzy's phone rang once, then twice, then three times. It went to voicemail. "Lizzy...pick up! They're here!" Kate whispered urgently into her phone. "ICE is here. They're right downstairs."

Suddenly Lizzy cut into her message and she took the call. Her voice was breathless. "Where are you?"

"In my bed. All the lights are out."

"Good—and where are they?"

"Down at the street. They're pressing the buzzer and yelling for me to let them in."

"Get under the bed or in a closet or something," Lizzy instructed. "Just hunker down in case they break in, and stay there until they leave. Don't turn any lights on at all today and stay away from the windows. And definitely don't leave. They'll be watching you, honey."

Kate began crawling along the floor on her hands and knees, phone still clutched in her fingers. "I know. Okay. I'm going under the bed right now."

"Okay, so baby, just remember. They want to scare you. They want you to feel threatened and to cave in, right? Remember we talked about this?"

"I remember." Kate curled into a ball in her spot under the bed. She pressed the phone against her cheek. Her heart beat wildly in her chest, and she breathed as deeply as she could, trying to calm down.

Lizzy continued in a matter of fact voice. "But you're perfectly okay. And you won't let them in, no matter what they say?"

"Of course not. Did you talk to Frankie?"

"This afternoon. But I'm calling the Peace and Justice people as soon as they open in a few hours. They're bound to let you in. I'll call you as soon as I know."

There was silence as Kate stifled a terrified sob.

Lizzy coolly continued. "So if they get in, you're not going anywhere unless a judge has signed their warrant. They wave papers at you, you have to check that, right? It's not legal otherwise. You've got a real one in your phone to compare it to. Shoot video if you have to."

"Yes, I've got it."

Lizzy took a breath. "Jesus. This is so fucked up."

Kate said nothing. She could only lie there and shake. "Help me find a place to go," she finally whispered, as tears began to roll down her cheeks. "Lizzy…I don't want to leave."

"You are not leaving," Lizzy said flatly. "Over my dead body, Kate. Anyway, I'm working on it."

"All right."

"Okay."

There was a pause, and Kate took a steadying breath as the pounding below began again. Once more the intercom sounded with a loud, rude jab of sound. "OPEN THE DOOR," the garbled male voice shouted through the intercom.

Kate closed her eyes. "Thank you, honey. I love you."

"I love you, too."

They hung up. Hugging her knees, Kate lay on her side and counted from 100 back to one to calm herself. She would get through this, just as she had gotten through every other test in a life chock full of tests.

She studied her waiting luggage, packed and ready, standing in front of the closet. She—no, the two of them—would get through this.

Thank God for Lizzy.

*

"Uh, hi…is this Monroe?"

Monroe hesitated and examined the caller ID on the phone once more. It revealed nothing more than an unidentified number in Oakland. The church secretary handed over the phone after calling Monroe upstairs from the sanctuary. "Who is this?"

"Sorry—it's Lizzy. From Driven. I'm your mechanic."

"Oh! Hey Lizzy." Lizzy was safe. That much Monroe knew. Lizzy and Tenika had seriously saved the day the last time Digby almost died. Digby was Monroe's extremely ancient Volvo. It had more than 250,000 miles and it was still going strong, thanks to the vintage timing belt they'd managed to find in some junkyard.

"What's happening, Lizzy?" Monroe heard Lizzy clear her throat. Something felt weird.

"So Monroe…I need your help," Lizzy began. Her voice sounded anxious and flustered. "I've got this girlfriend. Well, partner, really, even though we don't live together…yet, at least. Anyway, her name is Kate. I don't think you met her."

Monroe sat back and listened as Lizzy told her story.

"… then ICE showed up and started threatening me. Then they showed at her house, pounding on the door and trying to scare her, which is totally fucked. Anyway, I've got to get her out of there," Lizzy paused. "Monroe—you still there?"

Monroe was, but only marginally. *What was this all about, anyway?*

Lizzy's voice spiraled up enthusiastically as she finished with a flourish. "So I know you have a connection to the Peace and Justice Center, and I was wondering if Kate could get sanctuary there? I mean—any help at all would be *amazing!*"

Ah. There it was. Monroe cleared their throat. "Hey, listen, I'm sorry but we already have someone living here, Lizzy. A Mexican woman."

"You sure you don't have room for one more?"

"Let me check." Monroe covered up the church phone with a palm. "Rosemary?" Across the desk the church administrator looked up. "We're all full for sanctuary people, right?"

"Definitely," Rosemary said. "We only have one bathroom for a resident."

Monroe turned back to Lizzy. "Yeah. We're full."

There was silence on the other end of the phone. Monroe looked at the receiver. "Lizzy? You still there?"

"Oh…yeah." Lizzy's voice was subdued. She sounded

crestfallen. But then her voice cranked up for one more passionate pitch. "I've just got to say, Monroe, you're like my last hope. Every damn church in Oakland is full up with sanctuary people. Every last one. And if Kate gets deported, I'm going to..." Lizzy's voice faltered. Monroe just listened silently.

She continued after a beat. "Isn't there just some empty corner? I mean, Kate will sleep in a pew if she has to. She has like... no belongings. She's incredibly neat. Even just temporarily while I find her some place in...I don't know. Antioch! Or Humboldt, or wherever. 'Cause here's the thing, Monroe." Lizzy paused. "If I don't find a church for her, she has to go back to Ireland. And she can't go. She *can't*."

Now Lizzy was practically crying on the other end of the phone. "I love her," Lizzy finally blurted.

Monroe was silent. In all honesty, they didn't know what to say.

"I'll help you clean up the space if you have one. I'll do anything you want." Lizzy was now officially pleading.

Monroe began softly. "I wish I could help you. But we are full up. For real, Lizzy."

Lizzy sighed. "Yeah. Okay. I get it." Her voice dropped with dejection. "Thanks, Monroe. For considering it."

Monroe paused. There had to be something that could be done. Except that there wasn't.

"Good luck."

"Yeah. Thanks, anyway." Lizzy clicked off.

Monroe sat studying the phone. Moments like this massively sucked. Because there probably was some place for Lizzy's girlfriend to stay. The church was more than 150 years old, and loaded with obscure nooks and crannies. Monroe stood there for a moment, considering.

Yet it wasn't up to Monroe to decide who got to stay and who didn't, even if their official job was 'Facilities Manager.' This kind of thing was always the minister's call.

Shit.

There just seemed no possible way to help.

*

Two hours later, Monroe was playing Lauridsen on the small Hammond B3 in the chancel, and imagining the finely layered choral part. Monroe had spent the morning cleaning out the music loft up in the church tower. Mouse-chewed photocopies of Universalist hymns from the sixties had all been tossed, along with a few hundred mildewed editions of the more modern, teal-colored hymnal.

It was a long, dirty job and it was going to take the rest of the week. It even required a particulate mask because of all the mold up there.

Still, the view out the tall, arched windows over East Oakland always seemed to make things better as Monroe worked. These were Monroe's people—marginalized, pushed out by the gentrifying creep of White money and mores. Oakland was no longer a city owned by the Blacks, the queers, and the Latinx. Now, with the influx of tech money, their lives no longer seemed significant.

In came the so-called apothecaries selling expensive bitters and artisan whiskeys, the natty stores full of creative sneakers and hipster jeans, the kava bars, and the hot yoga studios. Even the ethnic eateries that had settled in East Oakland regularly attracted lines of Mercedes and Porsches, idling on a Saturday night as they waited for their tables.

Meanwhile, the working-class Blacks had already left in droves, gone to San Leandro or Antioch as the city slowly turned White. Where would Monroe go when the time came?

Solace was to be found in the music. That was the primary reason Monroe began hanging out at Peace and Justice to begin with. There was just something incredibly soothing about the drift of voices and piano up into the ancient redwood arches above.

That's why Monroe hung out here…for the odd moments in their day when they could sit down at the piano or the B3 and play. The church's sanctuary really did feel sacred somehow. It provided a respite in a city filled with shifting sands, and in a life that lacked a central organizing principle. The place was precious indeed.

Monroe was just swinging into the soaring third verse of "Dirait-on" when a thought came out of nowhere.

There is another bathroom.

Immediately, Monroe knew where it was. It hadn't been used for years. In fact, they had entirely forgotten about it. The tiny spare bathroom was actually only a few feet from where Monroe sat right now. Rising, Monroe walked over to the small outline of a door cut into the paneling at the edge of the chancel and turned the tiny, tarnished brass doorknob. The door swung open, revealing a dark space filled with cobwebs.

Monroe flipped the switch, but the light was broken. Still, in the gloom, they could just make out the space. Monroe now extracted a flashlight from a back pocket, turned it on, and scanned the space. There was a small sink and a toilet. Dusty old *Yellow Pages* telephone books from decades earlier were stacked up under the sink. An ancient toilet plunger lay on the floor. A huge cobweb festooned with dust hung loosely from the ceiling.

Monroe flipped one of the sink taps, and a trickle of rusty water began as the pipes shuddered and spat. Then a steadier stream of water began. Feeling emboldened, Monroe stepped further into the tiny bathroom and flushed the toilet. A rush of water filled the bowl.

The bathroom was small—just a toilet and sink—but it was working. There was no shower, which meant that if Kate stayed, she would potentially be an illegal guest of the church. And she'd have to share the shower of the other sanctuary guest, Catalina.

That was if Reverend Albiola would even agree.

Monroe stepped out of the bathroom and stood there for

a moment, hands on hips, surveying the vast, cool silence of the sanctuary. The huge, domed chancel had had its share of eccentrics in the pulpit over the decades. One of them, a White minister who was forever remembered for marching in Selma and spending two months in jail, liked to sleep in the church the night before he preached. Hence the Murphy bed. And the tiny bathroom.

Walking over to the tall, oaken door to the storage room, Monroe turned the doorknob. It opened with a creak. This obscure corner of the church was jammed as full as an overstuffed pocket. Sunlight filtered down from an arched window above a side door and spilled across a motley assortment of stored decorative items, making them look a little less dirty and forgotten than they actually were.

Much of the contents in here was junk at this point. Meaning it needed to be removed in the church-wide clean out that the Reverend had recently requested. Albiola Rendon, Peace and Justice's minister, was currently on a Feng shui kick, hence the mandate to get rid of all the old sheet music. If there was any space that needed cleaning out...well, it had to be here.

Here, in living color, were the remains of the last twenty years of chancel and altar decorations. Yards of tattered fabric were folded up in messy stacks on nearby shelves, while a profusion of faded, dusty fake flowers spilled out of tall paper bags stuck in the corners. An ancient cupboard, which had once contained clerical robes, was filled now with aging posters, thrift store vases, and candelabras. Behind the cupboard rose the outline of the former minister's Murphy bed. It was, in fact, still here.

A large carton of electric candles took up a central spot on the old marble floor. Monroe shoved it with the toe of a boot and it moved slightly. If Monroe cleared this space out, where would these things go? Perhaps the entire lot could simply be put into the dumpster.

Monroe stood in the doorway, considering the space. The

ceiling had to be fifteen feet high. More ghostly strands of old spiderwebs hung suspended in the sunlight, emphasizing the need for a good cleaning. Monroe chewed the inside of their cheek. It would take a radical overhaul right now—like…today. This morning, even.

The moldy music upstairs could wait, right along with the particulate mask.

If Monroe jumped on it now, Lizzy's girlfriend could maybe stay for a while until the next thing came along. The idea was empowering…appealing in its bald generosity. Monroe folded their arms across their chest and carefully ran through all the logistics of this transition.

Who knew what shape the Murphy bed was in, or if there was even a mattress? Lizzy would have to come on over and help move some of this stuff out of here, that was for sure. At the very least, Monroe needed everyone to help shove the massive oak cupboard aside. Even the minister.

Monroe now leapt into action, moving fast toward the office. Taking the stairs two at a time, Monroe hurtled ahead. A moment later, they tapped on the glass and peered into the administrator's office.

Immediately Reverend Albiola herself appeared. Apparently she'd overheard Monroe's conversation with Lizzy.

"Hey—did you know there's a bedroom in the—" Monroe began. But the Reverend held up her hand and smiled. She gleamed a little more than usual today, her shining eyes and her broad smile warming Monroe.

The Reverend Albiola's beautiful, bald, Black head cocked slightly at the sight of her facility manager's intense urgency. "I'm way ahead of you, Monroe," she said with a smile. "It's funny. I was wondering when we were going to tackle the chancel storage. Evidently, God would say that's right now."

Ten minutes later, Monroe was punching Lizzy's number

into their phone. Apparently the legality of the missing shower wasn't going to be a problem. For now at least.

"I think we might have a solution," Monroe began.

*

Lizzy regarded the manifest of the day's repairs and felt a wave of exhaustion overcome her. She hadn't slept since Kate's phone call the previous morning. On the other hand, Kate was probably still hiding under her bed, for all she knew.

Lizzy reminded herself that she didn't get to be tired. Not right now at least. Taking a long pull of the coffee in her travel mug, she shook off her malaise and went off to find a pair of new spark plugs.

Her phone buzzed in the pocket of her coveralls, and Lizzy took it out and peered at the screen. An unknown number in Oakland was calling her. For a moment she got the wild idea it might actually be a church calling her back. Lizzy stood stock-still as she answered.

"Hello?"

Suddenly there was Monroe, going on about a possible bedroom that could be put together out of a storage area. It even had some ancient Murphy bed in it, or something. But Lizzy was no longer listening.

Instead, she was already shutting off the lights and reaching for her helmet. She grabbed her wallet and spun around the closed sign on the garage door. Then stepping outside, Lizzy straddled her bike and took off as fast as she could.

Of course, she could be there in minutes.

Kate had found her sanctuary.

*

Rosalind stretched and yawned, willing herself to stay focused on the task at hand. It was day eighteen of her new job and she still had received no tasks, priorities, projects, or instructions from anyone.

Rosalind glanced at the clock on her computer. It was way too early to start yawning; that was for sure. Anyway, Rosalind had no reason to be so tired—except for the fact that she hadn't slept well since she'd overheard her two colleagues in the ladies' room.

No, she had to get focused. This was all there was to it. Rosalind took another long sip of the cooling black coffee in her paper cup.

Today's task was looking through old social media newsfeeds, and observing what was deemed fake news and removed by the company's AI bots. She was genuinely curious to see how these particular bots fared on the crowded feeds of their two biggest clients.

She scanned the feed archive of SpaceForAll, a social media stream that was their largest client. It was stuffed with last week's posts about everything from Katy Perry's extravagances to cauliflower pizza crust recipes and subtly inserted ads for animal print leggings. It all went by in a jumbled social whirl as her finger scrolled quickly along. The blur of the passing posts was hypnotic, but Rosalind kept going, figuring she'd eventually find her focus.

Here and there, a post highlighted in yellow spun by, signifying that it had been marked 'False Account' and effectively removed by the bots. She slowed down as she approached each one, taking them in lightly. The topics were the usual suspects. Hate rallies. Celebrity smears. False claims about pharmaceuticals. Anything to stir up trouble.

The minutes began to tick by as Rosalind scanned, and scanned, lulled by the utter repetition of the passing posts.

But then something made her slow down. Clearly the bots had missed one. Rosalind's mouse came to rest on a post of a news report about a new kind of discreet laser weapon, one used to attack the credit cards people carried and strip out the information. Rosalind stopped and read on for a moment.

Now, Rosalind opened a browser window and typed the name of the black ops laser system into Google. Nothing came up at all, except the SpaceForAll post she was already looking at. The laser information detection weapon didn't exist.

Clearly, the fake news bot had missed this particular post. Rosalind noted it, then kept on scanning through the thousands and thousands of posts that lay ahead. But now she was newly vigilant.

An hour later, Rosalind looked up and let the full impact of what she'd observed land on her body and her mind.

All in all, there had been twenty-seven missed fake news posts among the few thousand she'd just personally scanned through. It was an extraordinarily high number. So now she was left to wonder. Was the company's AI fake news detection system simply not market-ready? Or were those two women she'd overheard in the bathroom actually right? Was something more nefarious going on at this company that she had been left to stumble upon.

She replayed one of the women's comments: "Wait 'til Berring fills her in." Fills her in on *what*, exactly? Scott Berring was conveniently out of town at the moment, so Rosalind wasn't going to find out anything soon.

Now she recalled the last thing she'd heard as the women left the bathroom. It was something about how "fucking impossible" it would be for her to "remain neutral."

Sitting back, Rosalind considered what had just taken place. Clearly, this job was not what she'd been promised, nor even what it appeared to be.

So what was going on here, actually?

Rosalind had no idea. But she certainly intended to find out.

Chapter Eight

Lizzy bumped Kate's massive suitcase down the stairs as quietly and swiftly as she could. She heard the keys turn in the lock behind her as Kate let herself out of her apartment. Lizzy stopped and looked up the stairs at Kate.

"You ready?"

Kate sighed and looked at her, the air heavy with regret. "As ready as I'm going to be."

They continued on in silence toward Lizzy's waiting truck outside. It was just past three a.m., and the street was empty and silent, save for the electric hum of the streetlights. So far there had been no sign of ICE, or anyone else for that matter.

Monroe had agreed to let them in, once they reached the rear side door of Peace and Justice. It was the very same door that opened into Kate's new bedroom. Lizzy was looking forward to seeing how it looked.

She'd spent the bulk of the day there, helping Monroe move things around to make space for Kate and her belongings. The Murphy bed had been lowered, thoroughly cleaned, and made up. The bathroom with its tiny sink and toilet in the closet just off the chancel had been scrubbed and rid of numerous cobwebs. And something like sixteen garbage bags filled with tattered fake flowers, faded posters, and dead electric candles had been tossed out.

Lizzy and Kate drove on in silence. "You okay?" Lizzy finally asked.

"Me? Mm-hmm," Kate said lightly. But Lizzy caught a glimpse of her pushing a tear from her eye with the back of her sleeve. Kate was busy, as usual, keeping it together.

"Look," Lizzy rattled on, wanting to fill the space. "I mean, I'm just sorry we have to do this. There's no good reason for it."

Kate looked out the window as she tried to remain philosophical. "Well, it's my own fault. Or Mindy's...or, well, I don't know whose exactly. I suppose it could have been helped somewhere along the way. I certainly could have applied for a visa back when it was an easier thing to do."

Reaching a lanky arm over, Lizzy patted Kate's thigh. "Don't blame yourself, honey. It is what it is."

Kate just shook her head and stared out the window.

Now Lizzy cleared her throat. It was time to bring up the unmentionable, which she was really only marginally prepared for. Still, something told her it was now or never.

Lizzy's eyes studied the road as the highway unwound before them. "Uh, Kate?"

Kate's eyes found her in the darkness of the truck. "Yes, love?"

Lizzy took a breath. "I was just thinking...like...maybe we should just get married."

There. She'd said it. There was silence as the truck rolled along.

"You know?" Lizzy asked after a pause, her voice breaking slightly.

Kate said nothing. A few long moments went by, then finally, she spoke. "Now, Lizzy...love...I hardly think this is the time to have—"

"Hear me out, Kate, because this actually *is* the time. I mean...here's the thing: I know I should have asked you when I wanted to, back when you were living at my place. If I'd just gone ahead and married you, none of this would have happened, but—"

Kate's tone was gentle and reasonable. "If you had asked me to marry you then, Lizzy, I would have definitely said no."

Lizzy swallowed. Of course Kate would have. She already knew that.

"And now?"

Kate reached for Lizzy's hand in the cold, early morning air of the truck cab. "Lizzy. Sweetheart. I know what you're trying to do here and that is to keep me safe, and I truly do appreciate it. But the fact is, we're not ready to get married."

"How do you know?"

"I'm not ready," Kate continued.

"But …."

Kate turned to Lizzy, and her gaze burned a hole in Lizzy's consciousness. "Now is not the time," she said more firmly.

The truck pulled up to a stoplight, and Lizzy exhaled heavily. Then she looked over at her girlfriend. "I had to ask. To be square with myself. Anyway, I love you."

Kate kept her eyes straight ahead. "I know, love."

A pall of defeat hung in the air. "Anyway…" Lizzy said lamely.

"Yes," Kate said, agreeing to nothing.

A moment later, Lizzy pulled up beside the church's side door and glanced around. There was no one waiting in any vehicles, nor on the street. The exception was a tall, Black transvestite lingering in the shadow of the church alley, waiting to turn a few tricks from highway travelers passing through.

Lizzy and the prostitute eyed each other curiously. Then, Lizzy turned back to Kate, putting a cautioning hand on her arm.

"Wait—I forgot to tell you about Monroe. So just so you know, Monroe's a 'they.' Don't go calling them 'she.' Okay?"

"Fine. Thanks for telling me."

Lizzy got out and pulled Kate's suitcase from the truck bed. By then the door was opening, and the slight figure of Monroe appeared, looking a little ghostly in the middle of the night.

Immediately Kate seized Monroe's hand.

"Monroe! Thank you so much for doing this," Kate said as she was led inside. Before closing the door, Monroe glanced cautiously up the street. Then they locked the side door behind them.

"Glad you got here safe," Monroe said.

"Oh, you and me both."

Monroe looked slightly embarrassed now, as they gestured to the small space. "So…uh…so this is it, Kate. We're actually standing in your bedroom. I mean…I hope it's not too cold or too small or anything. Lizzy and I just had the afternoon to pull it together. But in a pinch…maybe it works?"

Kate looked around as they spoke, taking it all in. "I think it's perfect, and I'm sure I'll be just fine. I'm so very grateful. Thank you so, so much for making space for me, Monroe."

Monroe just smiled shyly.

There was an awkward beat of silence as the three of them stood there. Lizzy cleared her throat, and put her arm protectively around Kate. Then Lizzy and Monroe both began to talk at once.

"I guess I'll—" Monroe began.

"If we could just—," Lizzy said. Without further ado, Monroe left.

Without hesitation, Lizzy took Kate in her arms and kissed her deeply. "Every night I'm going to wish I was in here with you. And every day I'm going to visit you. And I'll call you. And text you. And…you know, all that stuff."

Kate was crying now, big tears rolling down her lightly freckled cheeks. She wiped at her tears futilely with her hands as if she were trying to gather them up. "That would be great…" she sniffed. "God, I wish you could stay here."

The church had made it abundantly clear that Lizzy was not to spend the night ever, under any circumstances. The two of them were expected to behave as if they were in a church—which they were.

"You and me both, but rules are rules—anyway, whatever. Here." She handed Kate her red bandanna, and Kate blew her nose. "Look, this is what we've been given, baby. We have to make the best of it."

"Yes. Of course, we will. I could be in handcuffs right now… Believe me, I know."

The two of them looked at each other sadly. "Yeah," said Lizzy softly, her voice breaking with emotion. "I'm so sorry."

"I'm the one who should be—" Kate began again, but Lizzy put a silencing finger to her lips.

"So that was then and now is now," Lizzy said. Then she paused. "This is just our new normal. And Kate—I'm sorry I proposed like that. I mean, driving to the church totally isn't the way—"

"No, Lizzy—stop." Kate shook her head. "You love me. I know that. You don't have to prove it to me."

Lizzy kissed Kate again. After a moment, Kate pulled back and looked at her. "And I love you." Then straining on tiptoes, she reached up and kissed Lizzy softly on her forehead. "Don't worry so, darling. You're going to think us both to death. Anyway, I'm going to be fine. You'll be fine. And *we* are going to be fine."

"Okay," said Lizzy, her own tears now beginning to collect. She wiped irritably at her eyes with the back of her hand, and gave a self-deprecating chuckle. "Damn. Guess we're both falling apart here."

They looked at each other for one more long minute.

"So…you'll be okay, then?" Lizzy asked.

"Yes. I already told you that, love."

"I'll come see you every day. And if you need any groceries, or anything just tell me."

Lizzy took a step toward the door, but then she turned back once more. "And Kate. I'm not going anywhere. I'll be here for you, baby. No matter what happens."

Kate just nodded, sniffing hard against her own tears.

"So…I guess I'll go," said Lizzy. Then silently, she went to the door.

Lizzy took one last look at Kate, standing there in the dim lamplight of her new, unofficial bedroom, the nineteenth century gloom of the church rising all around her. Kate was lovelier than ever, and so vulnerable looking in the half-light. Her strawberry blonde hair gleamed in the darkness.

"Well, bye then."

"Bye, love."

Taking a breath, Lizzy forced herself out into the chilly damp of a December night in the Bay. Intentionally, she began walking toward the truck in big strides, as once again tears ran down her face.

It was going to be a very long couple of months. Or however long this was going to take.

That's all she knew for sure.

The mini-skirted transvestite was now occupying a church doorway, arms folded against the cold as she scanned for cars in the distance. Lizzy looked over as she passed.

"Hey," Lizzy said softly, and the transvestite nodded in return. They were the only ones on the street.

Lizzy stopped for a moment. "You okay?" she asked.

"Mmm-hmm. It's freaking cold out here. That your girl-friend?" Lizzy nodded. "She's beautiful."

"Thanks. She's staying at the church," Lizzy said, nodding at the old stone building beside them.

"Sanctuary. She's Irish. ICE is trying to bust her."

"Wow."

"Yeah."

They stood there for another moment, sharing the silence. "Here." Lizzy pulled a five-dollar bill out of her pocket and handed it to the prostitute. "Stay safe," she said, and the transvestite nodded.

Then Lizzy got into her truck, sighed, and turned on the ignition.

A new feeling of uncertainty swam up her spine now and snaked out into her veins, leaving Lizzy overwhelmed. This had all been much, much harder than she had thought it would be.

What the hell am I supposed to do now?

Only days earlier everything had been fine—it had been better than fine. All that progress they'd made in counseling, and in simply spending time together had been so tangible, so real. It was a trustworthy love they'd developed over the last six months, one born of difficulties managed and truths told. Finally, things had gotten on solid ground.

But now, in an instant, all of that certainty was gone. Still...at least she'd asked about getting married, as awkward as it had been. At least she knew, with good clarity, just where Kate stood. The reality of Kate's reply now landed with a thud in Lizzy's system.

It wasn't great news that Kate had said no, but it wasn't catastrophic either. Kate wasn't ready. It was simply a fact, like rain was wet and sunshine was warm.

Lizzy took a deep breath as she picked up speed and pulled onto 580. She glanced at the clock. It was nearing four a.m. Still, steady traffic pushed forward all around her. It was simply the newest wave of early commuters heading down to Silicon Valley. Those who headed to work 'early,' to avoid the five a.m. slowdowns.

She shook her head at the absurdity of all of it. The traffic was just as inexplicable as Kate being locked up in a church. For a moment, Lizzy let herself think about their new reality. There would be no trips together across the Richmond Bridge to Rodeo Beach. No afternoon walks among the towering redwoods in Redwood Regional Park. There would be no Saturday morning wanders through the Grand Lake farmers market.

All of it was over. For now, at least.

Lizzy was just going to have to get used to the new emptiness. She pulled off at the exit for her apartment, and cruised through a yellow light off the highway. Beyond finding the right lawyer and working the system, Lizzy was now officially powerless.

There wasn't enough coffee, or cold beers, or work in the world to drown out the pure panic that now lived in her gut.

This was simply her new reality.

*

Kate bent to turn on the small, slightly bent, pink bedside lamp next to the Murphy bed. Then she contemplated the bed itself. A thin, lumpy mattress spread across the cramped twin bed frame, covered with a plaid blanket. The effect was less than appealing. She was exhausted but doubted she could sleep. Still, where else was she meant to go at this hour? Bed seemed the logical place. Even this one.

She was immediately grateful she'd brought her pillows and the thick comforter from her apartment.

Unzipping her hoodie, Kate pulled it off and stepped out of her jeans. She placed them on a stack of cardboard boxes in the corner, along with her shirt and her underwear. She shivered in the darkness of the church as the cold of the marble floor found its way up through her socks. Quickly she unzipped her suitcase and pulled out a pair of flannel pajamas.

Kate climbed into the pajamas gratefully, and then she gave the comforter several shakes to fluff it up again. She laid it over the blanket on the bed and smoothed it into place, just so. Kate yanked back the covers and inserted herself into the bed in one swift movement. Giving her pillows a quick pound, she snapped off the light, then she put her head down and burrowed for warmth.

Her eyes adjusted to the dark as she scanned the room around her. Indistinct stacks of plastic storage containers were piled in the corners. She could just make out the label on the one nearest her. "Altar Cloths," it said. There was a faint smell of old dust and cleaning solution in the air. *Mr. Clean*, she thought.

Kate sighed as she took it all in. What were the chances that she would have come to live in a church, lapsed Catholic that she was—and a queer one at that. She marveled at the sheer strangeness of it all as she lay there. What would her parents, devout Catholics themselves, think if they knew? It would give them a right laugh, that was for damn sure. Above her head, a peaked, stained glass church window towered over her, looking vaguely liturgical.

Kate rolled on her back and gazed up at the window. Lit by a streetlight, it appeared to be a scene of a family harvesting grain together. The grime across the colored panes of glass was obvious, but some words in ancient script were still visible. Kate studied them, but couldn't make out what they said in the gloom.

A slight draft from faulty leading in the window drifted her way, brushing across her cheek. Kate snuggled a little more deeply down under the comforter, even more grateful she had brought it with her.

She wondered, as she lay there, what she would do with her days and her nights here. A small, plastic card table with a flimsy cotton cover stood in the corner, along with a rusted metal folding chair. Above it was a faded poster that appeared to be from decades earlier. "Free Leonard Peltier," it said, above the face of a smiling, long-haired Native American man wearing a t-shirt.

This was only temporary, she cautioned herself. Nothing on this earth lasted forever—not even living in a sanctuary church. Things would shift and change. Perhaps Lizzy would find a lawyer who could finally, seriously help her get legal status.

On the other hand, maybe she would finally be forced to leave the church—and there would be her new friends from ICE, patiently waiting for her to set foot outside so they could send her home. Undoubtedly, they'd soon find out she was here.

Discovering the whereabouts of 'aliens' was just the sort of thing they were good at.

Kate closed her eyes now, letting the drift of sleep come closer to her jangled nerves. She thought of Lizzy's lingering kisses, and of her warm embrace in her bed, her arm casually resting across Kate's hip as they spooned together before drifting off to sleep. She thought of the first time she'd met Lizzy, back when she worked for Mindy Rose, and Driven was the competition she was supposed to be crushing.

Their entire history passed through her mind in a rapid sequence of images. Laughing. Kissing. Cooking together. Making love. Walking hand in hand along the streets of Oakland. Lizzy looking directly at her as she sang with her band, pouring her connection into that one direct, music-soaked gaze.

Still, marriage, right now at least, was most certainly out of the question. That much Kate knew.

Then there was the inevitable lurch toward Ireland that her mind always took at such moments. Back toward their disapproving looks when she tried to explain her queer life in America. And that she was a lesbian to begin with.

For Kate had never actually had that conversation with her parents. She'd never had the nerve. Da would just walk out of the room in disgust, and her mother would nervously change the subject to this nice young man or that nice young man as if she'd never said a thing at all.

That's what she'd be going home to, if ICE did manage to deport her.

Kate gave a long, low exhale, sinking a little more deeply into the mattress, which was arguably the worst one she'd ever encountered. She just hoped it didn't have bedbugs.

Please God, deliver me to whatever it is I'm meant to be delivered to.

Truly, she had no idea what that might be.

Chapter Nine

Rosalind sat in the driver's seat of her Prius, and considered her situation. Again, she reviewed all that she'd observed. And she considered whom she might talk to about it.

First, there was Scott, her boss. Who was not only out of town, but also likely the source of the shoddy AI in the first place. She pondered what his motives could possibly be, or if he was even aware of the flaws in the system.

He had to be. Scott was too smart, too buttoned up to not know that such huge lapses in the company's proprietary technology were happening.

For the fiftieth time that day, Rosalind considered the possibility that the flaws she'd found weren't flaws at all. And this was where it all became enormously tricky. If she'd stumbled upon some sort of black hat operation, Scott most certainly wasn't going to tell her about it.

Or would he?

Rosalind replayed the moment he had stood with his back to her on that very first day. He'd surveyed the view of the Oakland shoreline from the floor to ceiling windows of his eleventh-floor penthouse in his expensive, slate gray t-shirt. "Look around. Get to know the place," he'd said.

At the time, it had seemed an innocent enough invitation. A good idea, even. But only now was she beginning to understand exactly what he meant.

One of the two women she'd overheard had said it all. *"Wait 'til Berring fills her in. She'll probably be gone in a heartbeat."*

The truth stared out at her. The company could most definitely be running some kind of fraud, intentionally missing some of the more incendiary fake posts on the feeds they monitored. Perhaps they were even in cahoots with the large media companies they served.

But why would an alleged 'goody-goody' like her have been hired? And why would they intentionally want her to find out their scheme? And *who* wanted the fake news items to slip through the system in the first place? Was it Scott himself?

Rosalind lowered her forehead to the steering wheel and closed her eyes. Just this once, why couldn't her job be easy and straightforward?

Wearily, she opened the door and got out. Then opening the back door of the Prius, she leaned in and began searching the floorboards for the business card she'd tossed over her shoulder days earlier. It was the card for the psychic she'd been given at Driven.

A moment later, her probing fingers found the card tucked up under one of the seats. Standing up again, Rosalind looked at it.

Desire's Magical Garden
Tools for the Metaphysical Life
Psychic Readings

Rosalind glanced at her watch. Was she seriously going to do this? She'd never been to a psychic in her life. But something about the older blonde woman she'd met at the garage had been comforting. Reassuring even. Somehow Rosalind trusted her.

It was reassurance she badly needed right now. Rosalind took a deep breath and surveyed the card one more time, as if the answer to her troubles might be written on it.

Screw it, she thought. She'd just drive by the place. Then she'd decide then whether to actually go inside.

Ten minutes later, Desire's Magical Garden came into view. Immediately, Rosalind's stomach clenched at the idea of having her cards read.

This is a ridiculous waste of money, she told herself. *Get a grip.*

Yet, just at that moment, a white car pulled out of a parking spot directly across the street from the store. Before she could talk herself out of it, Rosalind pulled in to the curb and parked. Lowering the window, she studied the store. It was open.

Hell.

Without another hesitation, Rosalind did what she always did in such moments. She set her jaw, got out of the car, and walked into the shop before she could question herself again. She needed this. That's all there was to it.

Closing the door behind her, her eye took in the profusion of objects, old and new, arcane and ordinary, that filled the space around her. The place smelled slightly of incense and sandalwood, and the air was filled with sunlight and a slight layer of dust.

Quickly, her eye scanned the shelves of apothecary jars to her left, fully expecting to see Eye of Newt and Toe of Frog labeled among them. Instead, benign names of old, old herbs like comfrey and St. John's wort were neatly typed in place. This seemed oddly consoling.

A curvy, blonde woman with deep-set eyes was standing behind a high counter in the back. "Hi," she called out. "Can I help you?"

Rosalind stepped up to the counter and produced the business card. "Is the…uh…is this woman here?" she asked.

The woman smiled. "That me. I'm Sally." The psychic held out her hand, and Rosalind took it. Her hand was warm to the touch as they shook hands. Then Rosalind introduced herself.

"Would you like a reading?"

Dumbly, Rosalind nodded, as her mind sputtered in indignation. *What in God's name was she doing here?*

Instead of retreating, she surrendered her credit card. Then Rosalind followed the blonde psychic to a small, curtained room near the rear of the store.

They sat down at a round table covered with textured maroon velvet. The lamplight beside them was soft and golden, creating a circle of intimacy as Sally produced an aged, well-used deck of cards.

Thoughtfully, she handed them to Rosalind and requested she shuffle the cards. Awkwardly, Rosalind mixed the deck. A few cards popped out from her shuffling, and fell on the floor.

Rosalind leapt up to grab the cards, but Sally's hand stopped her. "I'll take those," she said pleasantly.

Sally picked up the cards and laid them on the table as she put the rest of the deck aside. Each card was decorated with a female figure in ancient dress. One said 'Yemanya' in decorative lettering, while the other said 'Diana.' Both were upside down in front of Sally.

Clearly Sally didn't use a tarot deck for her readings. Instead, Rosalind recognized the figure of Diana the Huntress, the Roman goddess of the hunt, with her poised bow and arrow. "What are these cards?"

Sally smiled. "Goddess cards. They help me lock in on what's going on, then usually my own visioning system takes over." Quietly, Sally contemplated the two cards on the table. "These two are actually important," she said.

Rosalind fell silent, waiting for further information. A moment later, Sally moved with certainty, offering her the rest of the deck once more. Rosalind drew ten more cards, and Sally spoke as she spread them out on the table. "Do you have a new career opportunity...or maybe a work challenge?"

Rosalind didn't reply, careful not to say too much.

Sally glanced at the array of cards before her, then she closed her eyes. "It doesn't matter, this job. Because this is not about the work. Instead, your own integrity is being called into question. This is really a test of your values. That's the most important part. You will always be tested, in every profession you choose, because you are a huntress just like Diana. And you're hunting for the truth."

She opened her eyes and looked at Rosalind. "Does that make sense?"

Rosalind nodded. It made too much sense.

"But don't be afraid," Sally continued. "Even if the opportunity seems clouded, it will lead to a higher sense of purpose."

"What do you mean by that exactly?"

Sally hesitated. "I mean that…well, let's see." Her voice drifted away for a moment. Finally, she took a deep breath and looked at Rosalind. "See this?" She pointed to a reversed card with the figure of the goddess Brigit. 'Don't Back Down,' it said.

"It's clear you're being tested. Someone is trying to find out if you'll support something you disagree with, perhaps something illegal. I'd say it's happening at your workplace. But Brigit is your defender. She's telling you to stay strong and get the information. To get in and get out, basically, and to be a warrior with what you learn. She's reminding you to do the right thing."

Rosalind was silent as a shiver moved down the back of her neck, and she tried to process what she was hearing.

Why did every last thing she tried need to be so difficult?

Sally continued. "Let me make this point again. This is a critical test for you, Rosalind. You have to take it, and you have to be brave. Like I said before, just get in, get the information, and get out." The psychic leaned in toward Rosalind. "This is much bigger than you realize. Potentially even at the level of national security. But if anyone can handle it, it's you."

"Oh," Sally continued after a moment. "Brigit is reversed because your tendency is to run away, to avoid conflict. To not make trouble. But not this time, okay? This is your moment to step up."

She smiled gently at Rosalind. "Does this make sense?"

Rosalind only nodded. Then the two women sat there in silence for another moment. "Any questions about any of this?" Sally asked.

Unexpectedly, tears now filled Rosalind's eyes. "No," she said hoarsely, sniffing hard.

Standing up, Rosalind reached for her bag, but Sally stretched out a hand. "Are you sure you want to leave? You paid for a full sixty minutes, Rosalind. Really, we're just getting started here."

Rosalind inched toward the curtained entry. "I'm sorry—I really have to go."

Sally looked at her with concern. "Do you have any support in your life? Any good friends to call?"

A tear now escaped Rosalind's overflowing eyes and rolled down her cheek, followed by another and another. Embarrassed, she stabbed at her now wet cheek quickly with the back of her hand. "I...uh...I have a meeting."

"It's okay," Sally said gently. "I understand."

"Thanks," mumbled Rosalind as she moved through the curtains as fast as she could. Obviously, Sally understood far too much.

"Come back anytime...even if you just want to talk," Sally called after her.

But Rosalind didn't reply. She just hurried for the door.

*

Sally slowly gathered the Goddess cards back into their box, contemplating her client's sudden departure, and the magnitude of what she had just seen. It was a many-headed Hydra that spread out in a million directions, spewing toxic anger and lies. The scale of the deception was enormous, touching thousands and thousands of people.

Sally had seen walls of fire, like a wildfire that swept into people's lives through their laptops and their phones. But the fire wasn't fire, per se...it was rhetoric. It was a million angry rants, pure hatred concocted to confuse and obfuscate.

Then, another vision landed and settled into Sally's consciousness—this one of Jack London Square. In it, she saw a lone shooter on a rooftop. A sniper, randomly killing people as they scattered and ran. The scene seemed indelibly real.

Sally took a deep breath, shaken by the vision.

The frightened young woman who'd just sat across from her was Hercules in this situation. Yet she was the only defense. Indeed, she was the best defense. She was the Chosen One whose job it was to tell the truth and slay the beast. For slaying the beast would, in the end, stop the sniper.

Sally couldn't even begin to imagine how the woman who'd just sat at this table was going to stand up to what was in front of her. Especially if she couldn't even stick around for the rest of the reading.

Breathing in slowly, Sally tried to calm her beating heart as she scanned the remaining cards on the table. Then slowly, resignedly, she put them back into the deck, shuffled them once and tucked them into their gold and yellow box. If only there was something she could do.

She didn't know where the woman worked, or even what industry she was in, though she knew her name. Really, it seemed like she worked in tech, or possibly social media. Still, it didn't matter. Sally had seen the destruction—the erosion of the public calm. The anguish. The blood.

She took another long, soothing breath. Anyway, wasn't this where she was supposed to pull down the veil? To stop feeling her client's pain and to quietly move on? Even if it did seem like it involved some sort of a major security emergency?

Theoretically, yes. But that was the part Sally didn't even pretend to be good at. She was terrible at detaching from what she picked up. Sally took another breath and began to feel her nervous system let go.

Couldn't she just get a little time on the job before all hell broke loose?

As she sat there, Sally thought about Frankie. Frankie would know what to do. Frankie always knew what to do when it came to matters of safety and security. But could Sally even discuss it with her? Technically, she was sworn to maintain client confidentiality. But where, exactly, was that line between client confidentiality and her responsibility to public safety?

What was intruding too much…and what was just plain being cautious?

Rising, Sally shook off her thoughts and slipped her deck of Goddess cards into the pocket of her skirt. There were books to price and sales to ring up.

For now, she would simply have to move on.

*

Rosalind got up and stared out the window at the lights beyond the Embarcadero. Over on Alameda Island, the tiny houses were dark for the most part in these middle-of-the-night hours. Stepping out on her balcony, she drew her blanket around her shoulders and hunkered down on the chaise.

In the sunlight, this chaise was her safe spot. Her recovery place. Her quiet corner in the storm. Even so, she'd never been out here in the middle of the night before. But the events of the day would not let her go. It was nearly two a.m. and she hadn't slept yet.

Again and again, Sally's words rang in her head, especially this part: *"This is your moment to step up."*

There was also that last, annoying comment. *"Do you have any support in your life? Any good friends to call?"*

No, and no, thought Rosalind. She hated the answer just as much as she hated that she'd been asked. Sally's apparent kindness simply felt like further validation of her failure in life to be a normal person.

Rosalind was going to have to be the hero, yet again, and she was going to have to do it all by herself as usual. Just like when she saved her grandmother from being swindled by the Chinese nationals running the blessing scam. If she hadn't come home early from school that day, her grandmother would have lost her entire life's savings.

Evidently that was early training for what was to come, if the psychic was right. The entire thing seemed far-fetched on one level. After all, how could one small security start-up, albeit with some very big clients, be doing something that affected national security? And what exactly did that mean, anyway?

After all, it was only social media True Wire was monitoring—not the Defense Department.

On the other hand, perhaps it was the smaller, lesser-known companies like hers that would be more vulnerable to infiltration, even by other governments. Especially if that infiltration was an inside job, engineered by the company's principals.

Back and forth she went, holding every fact she'd stumbled on, and every assumption she'd made up to the critical light of reason. Rosalind couldn't rest, basically, until she was done. She was already in way over her head.

"Just get in, get the information, and get out," the psychic had advised.

Everything Sally had said just felt so inexplicably right. And now here she was, staring at the dark contours of Alameda, unable to let it all go. Rosalind wished she'd stayed to learn more, for clearly this psychic had her finger on some kind of throbbing pulse of insight.

Whether Rosalind could stomach any more information was really the question.

Chapter Ten

Frankie took the steaming bratwurst on a bun and handed over the requisite cash. Then she headed straight for the sauerkraut. Forking a generous portion over Top Dog's finest, she hit the sausage with a top note of German mustard and walked outside.

Delaney, a Detention and Deportation Officer with ICE, was waiting by the curb, finishing up her own mango habanero sausage. Dabbing at her mouth with a paper napkin, she smiled a satisfied grin at Frankie. "Always a hit."

"Yep." Frankie took one bite of her sausage and then another. It was nothing less than a bun full of carcinogens with a chaser of grease, but she seriously didn't care. Top Dog fed her soul.

"Let's walk," Frankie said, taking another large bite.

"So, what's on your mind? Isn't every day I get taken out to lunch by the SFPD."

"This is on me," Frankie corrected. "Definitely not the department."

Delaney grinned at her. They'd known each other years earlier when they were both fresh out of the military, and newly landed in the academy. It was in the class called Accident Investigation where they finally met. Given that they were among the few butch lesbians in the place, they had an instant bond.

Three years ago, Delaney had transitioned over to ICE after one too many dustups with the powers that be. But she'd always been a little too outspoken for her own good. Or so Frankie thought. Quickly, she finished up her hot dog.

"So Delaney…" Frankie cleared her throat, and tossed her balled up, mustard-stained, paper napkin in a trash can as they passed by. "Can I count on you for some help?"

"Of course. Anything. What you got, Frankie?"

"I want you to do a little intel for me. That is assuming you want me to keep you in mango habanero Top Dog heaven."

Delaney chuckled. "You're damn right I do. What'll it be?"

"You got anything on an Irish expat who's been in Oakland for about seven years? Used to work for the racecar driver, Mindy Rose."

Delaney nodded her head, and made a small noise of recognition. "Yeah…it's funny. I was just looking at her file. Katherine something or other. She's not one of my cases, but I followed her former boss, Mindy, for a while. The big racecar driver—she did those tire commercials in a catsuit? Seriously hot stuff. Anyway, how'd you know about the Irish chick?"

Frankie shrugged. "Not important. You guys about to bust her?"

"Hard to say. She's got no record, but these days…" Delaney sighed. "I know there was one attempt, but they couldn't get her. Now she's got cover at the Unitarian church down on Fourteenth. She seems clean enough except for the immigration stuff…" Delaney's voice trailed off. She said nothing more.

Frankie looked at her. "And?"

Delaney shrugged. "And nothing. Not my case. Like I said."

"I got a lot more mango habanero dogs for you my friend…"

"If?"

"If you freakin' keep me informed."

"What's in it for you?"

Frankie chuckled. "Friendship. Nothing more." She gave Delaney a sidelong glance. "Why are you talking to me anyway, huh?"

"Why do you think? I miss the department. I've already told you that. ICE is like a dysfunctional high school where all the cheerleaders hate me. So if I can help a friend…"

"Exactly," Frankie concurred. "So we understand each other?"

"Affirmed."

"And you'll let me know if and when someone's going to bust her?"

"We can't bust her 'til she walks outside. Which she probably won't do anytime soon. And who knows how long enforcement will stick around? They're short-staffed as usual."

Frankie nodded. "Exactly what I was thinking."

The two women smiled at each other. It was good to have friends.

*

The Mexican woman stirred her coffee for the third time and contemplated the half-full cup before her, unsure what to say. Finally, she looked up at Kate.

"I feel like I'm floating," she said. "That's how it is after a while. You just float through life. Every day…" Her voice drifted off, but then she smiled. "I'm glad you're here. I need the company."

"I don't really know how long I'll be here," Kate hedged.

"You going back?"

"To Ireland? God, no! Well, at least I hope I'm not." Kate lowered her eyes and studied the tablecloth on the church table between them. "I guess it's not entirely up to me at this point, is it?" she added quietly.

"No. I get that point every time I walk out there." Catalina nodded to the door in the church kitchen. Outside was Castro Street, and just beyond that was an eight-lane highway, a high-speed conduit that was always loaded with traffic.

"You can't step past the bottom step of the stoop, but sometimes it helps. You know? Just to sit out there, see the sky. Hear the birds. There are birds, you know. Right here in the middle of the city."

Kate regarded the Mexican woman silently. Her face looked unbelievably sad.

"Pigeons. Crows. Grackles. Tough birds," Catalina continued.

There was silence. Kate took a sip of the coffee her new friend had made her. It was delicious, dark and strong. Then she cleared her throat. "What do you do all day, if you don't mind my asking?"

Catalina paused reflectively. "I circulate my online petition to stay. I'm hoping to get enough signatures to get a politician to put in a request for me. I teach people to make tamales. I do some yoga."

Kate sighed. The reality of her situation was now beginning to sink in.

"But don't worry, *flaquita*. You will find your way. You'll be out of here in no time."

"How do you know?"

Catalina shrugged, and her tone was straightforward. "You're a White girl."

Silence fell between them. Then the brown-skinned woman leaned forward on her heavy arms and gazed at Kate. "You alone, *flaquita*?"

"*Flaquita*…what is that?'

The woman suddenly laughed, and her eyes came to rest on Kate. "It means 'skinny little girl.'"

Kate smiled a little and shook her head. "Nope, not alone."

A look of delight passed over the woman's face. "You have a boyfriend!"

"Well, actually, it's a girlfriend. Her name is Lizzy."

Catalina smiled, her eyebrows raised. She nodded. "I like 'Lizzy'…that's a good name."

"She's a good person. An amazing person, actually. She found this place for me. I don't even know how she did it."

Catalina waved at the air around them. "God, did it, *flaquita*. You were meant to come sit by me and drink coffee and tell me your story. For now we will do sanctuary together."

Kate took a sip from her cup and she smiled. "Yes, I imagine we will."

"A nuestro destinos!" Catalina said, raising her coffee cup in Kate's direction. Kate smiled as they touched cups.

"Yes, indeed," she said.

*

The room of queer meditators fell silent as the large White man at the front of the room rang a small gong and sat back with a look of contentment. "Let's go in," he intoned. Scores of lesbian, gay, and trans people sitting on the floor on cushions or on folding chairs obediently closed their eyes. The practitioner's voice began its soothing stroll through their consciousness.

"Center yourself in your seat. Perhaps on your zafu or perhaps in your chair. Feel yourself settling into your place, letting the tension of the day drain from your face. Becoming still and quiet, this is your time to completely, totally, utterly let go…"

His voice was low and calming, and it almost took Lizzy by surprise. But then, a lot of things were surprising at the moment. Sally, who sat beside her in lotus position, had suggested they go to the Buddhist sangha together. When she heard about Kate taking sanctuary at the local church, she called Lizzy up immediately.

"Not a bad place to go when you're stressed," she explained.

Lizzy, who now had nothing else to do on a Tuesday night, readily agreed. After all, the Alphabet Sangha, so called for the wide variety of people in the LGBTQQI community who showed up, was something of a queer institution in the East Bay. Lizzy had never officially attended, nor had she *sat*, as the meditators referred to the 30-minute silent meditation that was the core of the practice.

Lizzy had no ideas if her knees or her mind could handle it. Still, if it would help Kate come back to her, she was game for anything at this point.

After several moments, Lizzy leaned over in Sally's direction. "How long is this going to last?" she whispered, but Sally didn't reply. A young, bearded trans man in a plaid flannel shirt turned around and shot her a look. Lizzy shut her eyes once more and tried again.

The problem wasn't that she couldn't concentrate. It was just her thoughts were entirely focused on Kate. For instance, where was Kate right now? Barely opening her eyes, Lizzy checked her watch. Two minutes had passed. Kate was probably eating dinner. Or maybe she was now washing up.

Someone named Catalina had apparently made her coffee and spent the entire afternoon telling her all about the place. Catalina had been in sanctuary there for sixteen months. In fact, Catalina might have even made dinner for her tonight. Kate even posited that she thought Catalina might be depressed.

Clearly they were getting to know each other.

Squaring herself on her zafu once more, Lizzy inhaled and tried to get back to nothingness. A thought intercepted: *what if Kate fell in love with Catalina?*

Was Catalina even queer? Hadn't Kate said something about her being straight? Still, all day long with nothing to do but wait might drive Catalina to be gay, at least for a while. It happened in prisons all the time, right?

Lizzy shook her thoughts off. *Trust Kate, you idiot*, she chided herself. Trust her as much as she trusts you. Because hey—here Lizzy was, surrounded by cute young things of all kinds. Lizzy opened her eyes and looked at the motionless meditators all around her.

Sally appeared to have not moved a muscle. Lizzy wondered if she was even still breathing. Gamely, Lizzy closed her eyes once again.

Monroe now came to mind. *Monroe.* If there was anyone she should be worried about, it was the fascinatingly ethereal Monroe, a 'they' if there ever was one. Monroe's wan countenance was maddeningly, alluringly non-gender-specific. That androgynous look was just the kind of thing Kate went for every time.

Damn. Why hadn't Lizzy thought of this before?

Now Lizzy's business partner, Tenika, flashed through her mind, and as usual she was not pleased.

What are you doing, girl? You acting all crazy again?

Yes, she most definitely was. All that had happened was that Kate had moved to the other side of town, and she was sleeping in a church at the moment. She was most definitely still her girlfriend. And even if they couldn't sleep together right now, they could text. And talk. And they could visit. And who knew—maybe Lizzy could sneak her out of there somehow. Or somehow even spend the night.

Kate would soon be talking to her lawyer about the case. Maybe the lawyer would even make a house call at the church. Maybe…

The gong sounded again, and the Buddhist monk's smooth-as-honey voice resounded from the front. "If you find yourself stuck, just let go. Remember, all of this is temporary. Life is temporary." He paused for a moment. "You are temporary as well."

Lizzy tried on this thought. *I am temporary.* She didn't feel very temporary. If anything, she felt like an old, well-used piece of furniture that was showing signs of wear. One way or another, she was going to get Kate out of there and safely back where she belonged.

She had to. That's all there was to it.

Chapter Eleven

Rosalind crossed her legs in the modern, uncomfortable chair in the hallway and folded her arms. She stared at the massive, six-foot-by-eight-foot photoprint of a cherry lollipop on the wall in front of her. Its enormous, candy red surface gleamed with a hint of saliva. Who knew this was art?

Rosalind had been waiting outside her boss's office for nearly forty minutes. She could see him through the glass walls to her right, pacing in front of his enormous window overlooking the Bay. Like all the other twenty-something tech millionaires, he was dressed in a gray hoodie, jeans, and creative 'sneakers' made of tweed and rubber. It was a look of studied casualness.

It was one of the rare days that Scott Berring was actually in the office. He was busy talking on the phone, as he had been for the last half hour. Occasionally, he'd glance through the wall at Rosalind as he paced around the office, phone in hand. Then he'd turn away once more, effectively ignoring her. But she didn't care. She was prepared to sit here all day if she had to.

Rosalind pulled her own phone out and did a quick check of nothing in particular. She was just biding her time, because sooner or later Scott had to emerge, whether to go to a meeting, or the bathroom, or lunch. She might as well wait him out, she reasoned.

Then she would finally begin to ask some questions.

*

Rosalind cleared her throat. After nearly two of the longest hours of her life, she'd finally gotten an audience with her boss. "Let's begin with the obvious, Scott. Why did you hire me?"

Scott leaned back and looked at her quizzically.

"It was a no-brainer, Ros. You were the most qualified person for the job. Why? What's the matter?" Her boss leaned across her desk congenially. "Here," he said, handing her a squeezable stress ball of the world.

She took it and examined it dumbly. Then she put it back on his desk.

"That's actually what we're doing here, Ros," he said.

"*Rosalind.*"

"Rosalind. Okay, whatever. We're all shaping and changing the conversation in America and the rest of the world. And we're doing it because we can."

Rosalind sat back in her chair and looked at him, unconvinced. "I don't think so," she said. "I mean, your system is flawed, Scott. There were twenty-seven missed fake news report in just the first two thousand I scanned. And I've found hundreds more since then. Are you aware of that?"

He shrugged and smiled. "No system is perfect."

"But this could be substantially better, Scott. Is there someone I can work with on this?"

He looked down at his hands, hesitating. Then suddenly he stood up and he began to pace. "Did I mention we just got our first fifty million? Round B was wicked," he said with a satisfied grin. "Gonna keep us all in gummy bears and craft brews for a long, long time. This train is moving forward, Ros, so you'd better get on board."

"Your system is broken, Scott."

He shrugged noncommittally. "Yeah, thanks. I'll mention it to Lester."

Lester Green was head of the software engineering team. It was his group that built and maintained the bots that monitored the news. Now Scott moved to the door of his office. "Gotta run," he said, nodding to the door in an indication it was time for Rosalind to leave.

"Seriously, Scott. Just please tell me. Why did you hire me?"

"Because I could," he said with a smile. "And I can tell you're gonna do great!"

"But great at *what*, exactly?" Rosalind asked, now blocking the doorway.

But Scott didn't take the bait. Instead, he just stuck his hands in his pockets and grinned at her, eyebrows raised. Then he shrugged, wordless.

Rosalind now walked away, unsure exactly what had just happened. The entire meeting had taken place in less than two minutes. Clearly Scott had no interest in correcting the errors, or even in hearing what she had to say about them. Or even telling her what her job was—or why she was there.

Yet, the performance of the flawed bots was basic to the entire premise of the company. Scott had just gotten fifty million dollars for technology that didn't even work.

A mild wave of nausea swept over Rosalind as she walked down the hall, and she felt nearly weightless. What was she doing here anyway?

Get in, get the information, get out, the psychic had said.

But…what information?

That was the thing that bothered her.

Rosalind stopped. She realized she was having one of those defining moments when life called you forth and you either stayed and engaged, or you tried to forget it ever happened at all.

Rosalind continued to stand stock-still.

It would be much safer, much easier, just all around better to drop all of this and leave the job altogether. Yes, she'd have to answer to her parents and herself on some level. For this had started out as a dream job.

Yet, her distress was real. It wasn't like she was going home every night with the glow of happy satisfaction. Rosalind frowned. There was nothing she could do to stop the chaos in this company, even if she did leave.

Or was there? That, of course, was the fifty million dollar question.

Slowly, thoughtfully, Rosalind began to walk the hallway once more.

Perhaps she just had to decide where to begin.

*

Monroe squinted at the sheet music on the iPad resting on the piano's music stand. Flicking through a few pages, they turned it off with a click and put the device aside. It wasn't time for Chopin or any of the rest of it.

Not right now at least.

Really, Monroe hadn't been able to focus much at all since Kate arrived. It was her very proximity, just on the other side of the chancel wall that was so uncomfortable. At least, Monroe assumed that's where she was. So far, Kate had kept a very low profile in the church.

Monroe sighed and studied the slightly yellowed ivory of the old Steinway grand. Their hands came to rest on the familiar keys, feeling their cool, smooth comfort. Once again, they began to play.

These days it was always the same piece. Undefinable—a genre unto itself that was both wistful and beautiful. Yet, it was untitled, too, for the piece hadn't been finished. This was what Monroe always did, begin things that could not be finished. Which is why, despite a music degree from Oberlin, Monroe's days were spent playing the piano and cleaning out obscure corners of the church.

The simple melody drifted up into the huge, vaulted ceiling and mingled with the massive redwood rafters above. Each one had been cut and shaped 150 years ago, back when California was new, towering trees were abundant, and anything seemed possible. Now, the few old-growth redwoods that remained were protected, and Oakland was all traffic, money, and crowds—the very things that Monroe couldn't tolerate.

Which explained why Monroe spent nearly the entire day, every day, knocking around the darkened sanctuary of the church. Here it seemed quiet and safe. Or it did until Kate arrived.

There was a rustle in the back of the sanctuary, and Monroe, fearing it was Kate, immediately stopped playing. The figure came up the aisle toward the chancel now.

"Please don't stop. That was lovely." It was, indeed, Kate.

Monroe swallowed hard and tried to contain the profuse blush that was spreading across their face. *Shit.*

"Hi, Monroe. I don't want to interrupt you," Kate said.

Yet, here you are, walking toward me. Practically swinging your gorgeous hips in slow motion.

Monroe managed to fumble a few words, before turning back to the piano. "No…uh. It's okay. It's fine. It's…yeah." Monroe now fixed a gaze on the music in front of them as they tried to ignore the beating of their heart.

Monroe shifted on the piano bench, wishing like hell Kate would just vanish. Instead, Kate sat down a few feet away in the first pew. Monroe noticed she was wearing a lavender button down blouse and a pair of perfectly fitted jeans.

Kate was so beautiful, so delicate, sitting there in the shafts of sunlight that poured down from the old stained glass windows. Her long hair was a shade of golden reddish blonde Monroe had never seen before. It was the kind of hair you could run your fingers through for hours on end. Monroe did their best not to sigh with simple appreciation.

"Go on," Kate said, nodding toward the piano. "If you don't mind me listening."

"Oh." Monroe looked at their hands, as if willing them to play. Somehow these same hands that were making sweet music only a moment earlier were not cooperating now. Instead they stayed frozen on Monroe's lap. Yet again, the inner turmoil began.

Play the damn song. She wants you to.

Monroe hesitated. Despite all those Sunday mornings of playing on cue at 9:15 and again at 11:15, everything had just slid into breakdown.

She's going to walk away thinking you're a total idiot. Come on, just play the damn song.

After a moment, Monroe began to gently play the melody with one hand. In their peripheral vision, they could see Kate smile. She listened quietly in her pew.

Monroe took a deep breath and put both hands on the keyboard, finally sliding into the well-practiced grooves of the piece. Lilting piano filled the air as Monroe picked up steam. Now, the bigger chords began. A suspended seventh chord hung in the air and then resolved into an unexpected bridge.

Playing for Kate, as she sat there in the sanctuary, listening peacefully, was strangely profound. It had an unaccustomed intimacy Monroe wasn't used to. For the fact was that no one ever listened to Monroe's most private, original pieces. Mainly because Monroe never shared them.

Finally, the liftoff of the final chorus began. This was the climax of the piece, as it hurtled toward its big, chord-rich, crashing conclusion. But then suddenly everything stopped. Monroe once again removed their hands from the keys.

Monroe's cheeks flared red once more. "That as far as it goes." Monroe looked at their hands once again, unable to even glimpse in Kate's direction. Never had they felt so entirely, absolutely naked.

"It's incredible. It's…" Kate began. She was visibly moved by the music. Kate stood up and walked toward the piano. Then pausing beside it, she ran her hand on the softly aged black surface of the piano.

"Wow. It's…" Kate stopped, unable to come up with the word. "What's it called?" she finally asked.

Monroe was still head down, eyes on hands. "I don't know."

"You don't know?"

Now Monroe looked directly up at Kate. The sight of her was entirely overwhelming. And breathtaking. "I haven't titled it yet."

Kate's eyebrows shot up. "You *wrote* that?"

Monroe nodded, embarrassment practically oozing out of every pore. This conversation was becoming excruciating.

"Oh, my," Kate gushed. "You are—well, you're a bloody genius is what you are. Clearly you're very gifted. Have you recorded your music?"

Abruptly, Monroe stood up. "Actually, I've got to go." Gathering up the iPad, Monroe tucked it under an arm. "Bye," Monroe said, turning toward the side door of the sanctuary.

"Wait!" Kate called as Monroe hurried away. "Monroe!"

Reaching the safety of the doorway, Monroe dared to stop. Pausing, Monroe turned and looked back at Kate. "Thanks for listening."

Kate said something, but Monroe missed whatever it was.

It was seriously time to go.

*

Frankie brought Sally's wrist to her mouth and kissed it tenderly. She loved this wrist, fleshy and ripe, and the long fingered hand attached to it. Sally's body was an endless discovery for Frankie, as their lovemaking continued to unfold, getting better and better as the months wore on.

Yes, she loved Sally's fleshy, tender wrist. But did she love

Sally herself?

Probably, Frankie told herself. Propping herself up on one elbow, she looked at her lover.

It was a perfect Wednesday afternoon. The sun was out, it was unseasonably warm, and the pre-Christmas rain had abated for now. Everything in their midst was warm sunshine and ease like melted butter. It was an afternoon to get lost in.

Sighing, Frankie leaned over and kissed Sally's delicious lips. It felt so good to finally relax. Amazing, even. Sally responded, her tongue sliding easily into Frankie's mouth. They kissed. And then they kissed some more.

Moving across her lover's body, Frankie lowered herself over her and once again began to find her way inside her. They'd been here for hours. But then, that's what they did. They made love, and they talked. Then they made love some more.

They eventually got up and went out for tonkatsu ramen, or dosas. Or dumplings. Or tacos on homemade tortillas. Or a light-baked Arizmendi pizza they finished in Sally's oven and ate naked in bed. All of it was chased down with a really good, oaky Chardonnay, or perhaps a wintery Cab. At the moment, they were liking the one called Ménage à Trois.

"Honey?"

Frankie pulled back slightly. "Mm-hmm?" She did not stop what she was doing between Sally's legs, but instead of opening up to her, Sally was now pulling away. She sat up.

"Let's go out," she said.

"Wait—really?" Frankie looked up at her. Sally had a look on her face that Frankie hadn't seen before. She put her hand on Sally's thigh. "What is it, honey?"

Sally hesitated. "Oh, it's nothing. Everything's fine. I just..." Her unfinished comment drifted away as a cloud now covered the sun. In an instant, the afternoon glow had shifted to the flat light of threatened rainfall.

"Tell me," Frankie urged. "What's wrong, baby?"

Sally laughed and shook her head. "Really, it's nothing. I'm hungry!" she announced. "Let's get out of here." Sally rose and went into the bathroom.

Somehow Frankie doubted this, but she went with it, following the sudden shift in the tide. She tried not to worry as she sat up and reached for her undershirt. After all, they'd been making love for nearly an hour.

Maybe this was the beginning of phase two—the settling in. That's when all lesbian couples finally got out of bed and started assembling a life together.

Yeah, that was probably all that was happening.

*

Down the hall in Frankie's bathroom, Sally sat on the toilet and put her face in her hands. It had been several days since the reading with Rosalind, but still she couldn't get it out of her mind.

The problem was that the information just kept on coming, just like water trickling through a leak in the dam. It filled her head, and her senses, and every so often it lit up her brain with images of ongoing destruction. Apparently the message had been delivered for her just as much as for Rosalind.

Which was exactly why Sally hadn't done readings professionally until now. Somehow she'd known this was exactly what would happen.

Couldn't she just enjoy spending the afternoon in bed with her girlfriend?

Apparently not. They were bugging her again, relentlessly now, agitating for her to tell Frankie about her visions. They, of course, were the vaporous spiritual beings, energies, or ghosts, or apparitions, or spirits—or whatever you wanted to call them—that lined up around Sally and constantly whispered in her ear.

They were also the very beings Frankie wanted nothing to do

with. Frankie didn't believe in spiritual entities, regardless of the fact that they were making her girlfriend's life a living hell.

Sally had tried to make the spirits go away. She'd brought home not one but two candles for protection from Desire's, lit them both, and put them on the mantel in the living room she shared with Delilah and Tenika. Regularly, she stopped beside them and chanted this incantation or that.

She'd prayed. She'd done a ritual clearing. She'd cleansed all of her crystals, including her moonstone pendant and earrings. She'd even smudged the hell out of the apartment with a bundle of sage given to her by a local Miwok woman. It made Frankie sneeze.

Sally was doing every last thing she could to make the insistent messages go away. Yet, still they lingered. She looked at herself in the mirror. She should just tell Frankie about the reading, and the messages she was getting. Wouldn't she want to know if Sally or anyone else was in danger?

Yes…but to Frankie at least, this would not be seen as a clear and impending threat. This was just someone else's psychic reading now playing interference in Sally's brain. If nothing else, for reasons of client confidentiality, Sally needed to leave it all alone.

And yet…there was still that sense of imminent doom that she just couldn't shake. It was those fragments of hell she kept seeing: the bleeding bodies strewn around Jack London Square. The anger explicitly spelled out in videos and texts, and all the people responding to news of the fake rally. They'd come bearing signs, holding their sons and daughters by the hand and wearing sunscreen, expecting to express their opinions aloud.

This was the knot in Sally's stomach that refused to go away. Worst of all, there was that damn message Sally heard again and again from her guides: *Tell Frankie now.*

It wasn't just 'Tell someone'…or even 'Tell the police or the FBI.' It was painfully obvious what the spirits wanted her to do.

Sally stood up and went to the bathroom door with new resolve. She would share what was happening inside her rattled psyche. Even though she already knew what her lover would do. Frankie would look at her skeptically, eyebrows raised. Then she would abruptly change the topic.

But then Sallly paused, hand on doorknob, and reconsidered. Almost certainly, Frankie would automatically disregard anything she said. And that would be just too painful to bear.

No, on second thought, she'd say nothing. Sally couldn't tell Frankie—not now, at least, when they were finally becoming closer.

She would simply have to find another solution.

Chapter Twelve

"The corn husks take about two hours to soak, so I start them early, right?" Catalina's chunky, brown hands lifted the wet, pliable corn husks from the sink they had been soaking in and put them in a strainer to dry.

Her movements around the kitchen were swift and focused. Catalina had clearly done this hundreds of times. But that's who she was—The Tamale Lady, as they called her in Temescal. A local, beloved figure who'd sold handmade tamales from her food truck for years.

Kate watched her work, somewhat spellbound.

The handful of dried cascabel chiles Catalina had split open and stripped of seeds had been boiling for a while now, and a pungent smell of dried spice and garlic hung in the air. Soon these would be blended into the sauce that would make the tamales sing. "My favorite part," Catalina said of the blend. The mixture was dark, red, and thick like blood, and it was dense with the smell of chiles.

Fifteen minutes later, Catalina was up to her wrists in a large metal bowl of corn masa. Kneading it with her hands, she broke it down, squeeze by squeeze. More chile puree went into the masa as she kneaded on and on. It was an *accent*, Catalina said. Minute after minute, her strong, brown arms worked the stiff dough. "Here's where you've got to sweat!" Catalina laughed, pushing a stray strand of black hair from her face with the back of her hand.

Now she let Kate do some of the work. Pushing up her sleeves, Kate plunged her hands into the mixture and felt the masa crumble and break down as she mixed. Moving the dough around was like pushing at a heavy rock. "Like this, turning the bowl," advised Catalina as Kate kept on grabbing at the dough.

"This is hard work!" she said, a little breathlessly. Kate kept at it for what seemed like an unreasonably long time, until finally the masa began to loosen up in her hands.

Catalina smiled. "Work for strong women."

Eventually the masa was smooth, flat, and slightly shiny. Catalina peered over Kate's shoulder.

"Perfect! You're a natural *tamalera, flaquita.*"

Now Catalina began to spread the mixture inside some of the corn husks. Then she filled each tamale with seasoned, shredded pork that had been stewing in a slow cooker. She folded the tamales up into tidy corn husk packages. "Come on!" she encouraged. "You can do this. The hard part is over, *flaquita.*"

Awkwardly, Kate tried to replicate Catalina's sure moves, but the filling squeezed out of the ends of her package. Clearly this was trickier than it looked. After a moment, she stopped. "I think I'd rather just watch you," she said and Catalina shrugged and smiled shyly at her work.

Kate could clearly see her friend was in her element, humming along in a well-practiced groove. Even in the confinements of Sanctuary, Catalina seemed to have a purpose.

Eventually, she turned to her massive aluminum *vaporera,* sitting on the stove. Clearly the old steaming pot had seen a lot of use. The sides were dinged and slightly battered, but the lid still fit tightly. Kate watched as she filled it partly at the sink. Then Catalina dug some spare change from the pocket of her apron and threw it in the bottom of the pot.

"What's that for?" Kate asked.

"Like an alarm. When I hear the money jingling, I know there's enough water in the pot."

Kate smiled. Clearly Catalina was an old pro at this. Sitting back, she marveled at the sheer volume of what was being produced. "How many tamales are we making?"

"A lot!" Catalina laughed. "I got people out there. They *always* want tamales."

Kate watched as Catalina swiftly inserted the tamales into the huge steamer. A few minutes later, an army of tamales filled the pot in a tight spiral. Packing the bundle with a layer of corn masa, Catalina then stopped and bowed her head briefly. She made the sign of the cross over the tamales, then she put on the lid and turned up the heat.

Catalina smiled at Kate. "Never hurts to bless them," she said.

Soon the kitchen was rich with the aroma of steaming pork, tamale, cumin, and chiles, and Kate savored the smell. It had been a long time since she'd cooked with anyone, or even smelled simple, well-made home cooking like this. So far, she'd been living on bagged salads, yogurt cups, and microwaved Trader Joe's dinners that Lizzy brought her each week.

There had been several such visits from Lizzy so far, and Kate hung on to them for dear life. She needed Lizzy more than ever, that much was clear. Yet, at the same time, she was retreating into herself somehow. The walls of this church provided a sanctuary, yes. But they also put a division right down the middle of their relationship.

Lizzy was out there, and she was in here. There was no way around it. Nor was there any end in sight.

Now, well into the second week of sanctuary, Kate was clear on this much: this was no place to have a relationship with the outside world at all. It was as if a little more of her energy was being sucked into this church every day. She wondered if she was becoming depressed.

"You're quiet," Catalina observed.

"I'm sorry…I'm just thinking about things."

"Your friend."

"Well, yes, Lizzy. But I don't know… I feel this church is already taking something from me. I mean, I'm so grateful to be here. You know I am, but—" Catalina held up a silencing hand. Then she smiled sadly at her new friend.

"This is what happens," she said. "Somehow this place owns us. It just does. And our only choice is to surrender, *flaquita*. That is all we can do."

Surrender.

This was not welcome news to Kate. "But I'm really just passing through. I'll be out of here eventually, when—"

Catalina smiled. "When your lawyer calls. That's what I thought, too." Striding over to the oven, she opened it and peered at her baking tamales. Then she shut it, apparently satisfied. Catalina turned and faced Kate. "And I'm still waiting eighteen months later. We must fill our days with something other than hope, *flaquita*. It's better to focus on what is happening right now."

Kate took a deep breath and considered what Catalina was saying.

She couldn't wait for Lizzy to get there.

*

"Hey, hey—what's this?" Lizzy began, leaning in for a hug.

Lizzy happened to knock just as Kate was lying on her Murphy bed, staring at the stained, vaulted ceiling above her head. The chilly winter gloom of the dirty church window above her reinforced her captivity. It could have been covered with iron bars or not. The effect was the same.

Kate wiped the tears from her face as Lizzy stepped into the church. She shook off her rain-drenched slicker and hung it on a nearby hook. Then Lizzy picked up the bouquet of cheap roses she'd brought with her. She held them out a little awkwardly. "Here," she said a little stiffly. "For you…cause…you know."

"I'm sorry, honey," Kate said, blowing her nose. She sighed heavily, not taking the flowers. "I'm just…" Kate couldn't finish her sentence.

Lizzy put the flowers down on the bureau, as Kate sat up. She took Kate in her arms. "Looks like I showed up just in the nick of time."

Holding on to Lizzy for all she was worth, Kate dissolved. She began to cry in earnest into the soft flannel of Lizzy's shoulder. Shaking with sobs, Kate let go of all she'd been holding back for the past several days. Wordlessly, they stood like this for a while.

Kate kept meaning to stop crying, but she couldn't. Finally, Lizzy led her over to the bed and they lay down together. Lizzy spooned her lover from behind. "Come on," she kept saying, curling her body into Kate's. Again and again, she stroked Kate's arm. "You're going to be okay. Come on…I'm here."

"I'm not going to be okay—I'm not!" Kate sobbed. "I mean, I appreciate that you're here, but I'm getting sent home, Lizzy. You know it and I know it."

"Who said this? What do you mean?"

Kate sat up and looked plaintively at her girlfriend. "Anyone can see it, Lizzy. So why can't you?"

Lizzy rolled onto her back. "Because it's not going to happen. Everything's going to be okay, Kate. It really is."

"Okay, fine. Whatever." Kate lay down in Lizzy's embrace once more. She clung to the flannel shirted arm around her, pressing her wet face into Lizzy's hand. There was silence for a long time.

After a moment Kate spoke. "Honey?"

"What?"

"What if you came to Ireland? Just let's go back. We'll find work. We'll start all over again together. That much we know we can do. You can get papers. It would be far easier than me staying here."

Lizzy stroked Kate's red, swollen face. She smiled a bitter-sweet smile. "I would if I could, baby. But you know I can't do that. Everything I've got is tied up in the garage. Everything."

Kate gave a heavy sigh. "Right. The garage."

"Kate," Lizzy said plaintively. "It's what I do."

"I know, I know." Kate sat up and blew her nose grumpily. "Of course, you could open a garage in Ireland. But, whatever…"

"What's your lawyer say?"

Kate looked at Lizzy. "Nothing. Not one damn thing. Which probably means exactly nothing is happening. *Dammit!*" She slammed her fists down on the bed. "This is so unfair! Why the hell did I have to get targeted—what did I do? I've never gotten so much as a traffic ticket!"

Lizzy was silent for a moment. Finally she could contain herself no longer. "Well, sweetheart, you know what I think you should do."

Kate threw her hands up in the air. "Lizzy, I *know* what you think I should do, and I've told you—" she began in exasperation, but then she caught herself. She stood up. "Look, I realize you're just trying to help, but even locked up in here I'm not ready to marry you."

Lizzy was now lying on her back, with her hands behind her head. She studied the ceiling. "Okay…okay. It was just an idea."

Kate continued, relentless. "I know what you're thinking, Lizzy. *If only Kate would just get with the program and marry me everything would be just fine.* You *know* you thought that…"

Lizzy looked at her. "Is this seriously going to help right now?"

Kate began to pace around the tiny bedroom. "Pushing and prodding at me has never helped before, Lizzy, and it won't help now. I'm sorry, but this is who I am and I can't be made to be someone other than me." Her voice rose up and she was shrieking. "I'M MOVING AS FAST AS I CAN, GOD DAMMIT."

Lizzy sat up and looked at her girlfriend as she ricocheted back and forth across the small, dark space. "Kate, honey…I think you need to chill out."

"YOU CHILL OUT!" Kate suddenly stopped and whirled around. "Just…go home, Lizzy. I'm sorry. This is not a good time."

Lizzy blinked and sat up. "What?"

"Here." Kate handed Lizzy her backpack. "Please leave."

Slowly Lizzy stood up and took her backpack. "Are you okay?"

Kate looked at her furiously, her hands on her hips. "What do you think?"

"I think you're a basket case." Lizzy studied her girlfriend. "You seriously want me to go? I mean, I just got here."

Kate just stared at her. After a moment, Lizzy reluctantly slid the backpack on her shoulder. Wordlessly, she looked at Kate. Then she touched her arm. "I know it's intense, Kate. I can only imagine, really, but—"

Furiously Kate yanked back her arm, marched over to the door, and pulled it open as sheets of rain began to blow in the room. "Just go," she said, pointing out to the deluge on the street. "Leave."

"I—" Lizzy began, but then she stopped. She sighed and putting down her backpack, pulled her rain slicker back on. Sadly, she went to the door. Then she turned to face Kate. "I'll check in on you tomorrow."

"Don't bother."

"What did I do?" Lizzy asked from the doorway. Then she shook her head. "Actually, don't even answer." Turning she headed out into the rain as the door closed with a thunk behind her.

Kate stood now looking at the closed door. Once more, she ran her hand over her tear-stained face, and she gave a sigh. "Shit," she murmured as she lowered herself shakily onto the bed. Once again, she began to sob in earnest.

What have I just done?

She really must be falling apart.

*

Frankie put the vibrating pods down and looked at her therapist. "Is this actually even working?"

Silently, the therapist shut off the small EMDR machine in her lap. "Well…do you think it is?"

"I'm asking *you*, doc. Fucked if I know. I mean…*maybe* it is?"

The therapist sat back against her chair and regarded Frankie placidly. "What would you like to accomplish here, Frankie?"

"I want to feel closer to my girlfriend. I want to love her."

"So how's it going?"

Frankie leaned back and shook her head. "I don't know—maybe I do? I mean, lookit. She's a psychic. That's a huge problem for me. You know it is."

"Mm-hmm."

"But that seems like a stupid reason not to be all in. The thing is…I…" Frankie looked up at the therapist. "I'm not all in. I mean, maybe I'm small-minded or a bad Californian or something, but I'm a cop. And it's like—when you're dead, you're dead. You know what I mean?"

The therapist just looked at her sympathetically.

Frankie's voice took on a note of pleading. She'd had just about enough of this half-in-half-out relationship. In fact, it was driving her crazy. She had no idea whether she could even trust Sally at this point. Though Sally, in and of herself, had done little to erode Frankie's trust.

"Doc, please. You've got to help me here."

The therapist put her notepad down. "Maybe the relationship is simply not meant to be," she suggested gently.

"Oh, no. Now, wait a minute, here. We are not going backwards, doc. How many of these damn sessions have I done already?"

"You can't force love, Frankie."

"Yeah, yeah. Okay. I hear you." Frankie sighed. Then she sat thinking, as the clock ticked on across from her. Finally, she spoke.

"Do you suppose I actually do love her?"

"You tell me. Do you?"

"Well, I'm not giving her up. Not yet at least." Frankie paused. She thought of the numerous women who wouldn't date her because of her own profession. "Breaking up because of someone's job is a stupid fucking reason. I actually know something about this."

The therapist looked pointedly at the clock. "We'll talk more next week," she said.

Frankie rose as a small wave of gratitude washed over her. "Thanks, doc," she said. "That was definitely the right question."

It was good to have a rudder in the big, wild sea in front of her.

*

Sally sat bolt upright in her darkened bedroom as a small, terrified sound left her body and a nightmare woke her. She wondered for a moment if she was having a panic attack. Slowly, her breathing returned to normal as she looked around her at the reassuring, the familiar.

Beside her, the clock blinked that it was 2:45 a.m.

Lying back down again, Sally rolled on her side and closed her eyes. Taking a deep breath, she began to methodically relax every muscle in her face. She released her tongue from the top of her mouth. Then she moved on to her jaw, loosening it from the tense grip it often held at times like this.

Sally's anxiety was as old as the hills, and just as entrenched. She took a long, deep breath. Sometimes, there was just no talking it down. Really, all she could do right now was to let go and surf the images that came to her.

In this particular dream, her spirit guide was staring at her upside down, its eyes intensely focused on her. Its gaze demanded her absolute, complete, and total attention. Sally's spirit guides didn't usually mess around, and this time they were being alarmingly clear.

Tell her, they said. *Tell Frankie what is going on.*

Sally rolled over, doing her best to smother the thought with her own racing mind. No, she would not be telling Frankie, just like she'd informed her guides yesterday. And the day before.

This was when she usually reminded herself they were only images in her head. Even if now they'd taken to hanging upside down in front of her. Was it really worth it to risk being dumped by the first girlfriend she'd felt seriously connected to in forever?

Then Frankie would just become another sad statistic—GF number thirteen to be specific. And that just plain sucked.

No, Sally wasn't rushing to tell Frankie what she'd seen in Rosalind's reading for about seventeen different, excellent reasons. Instead, she would continue to maintain professional silence, and she'd bide her time. Why in the hell her guides couldn't understand this, she didn't know.

Sally rolled over once again and hugged a pillow tight to her chest. Once again, she relaxed her brow, her eyes, her cheeks, her jaw... Then, a thought struck her.

Maybe she should invoke the *Bless it or Block it* prayer. She could at least do that, right? It would be a form of compromise.

Fine. All right. It was the correct thing to do.

Now, Sally rolled on to her back and stared at the ceiling above her. Centering herself, she spoke her prayer aloud into the darkness of the empty apartment. "God, please help me learn whether to tell Frankie what I saw in Rosalind's reading. If you want me to do this, please bless it. Or block it if you don't. Show me a clear and obvious sign, please."

Then returning to hug her pillow once again, she closed her eyes and finally, mercifully, found herself drifting back to sleep.

Four hours later, Sally walked over to the kitchen cupboard and extracted her box of Lemon Ginger tea bags. Beside her the kettle began its high-pressure scream. She snapped off the burner and pulled a tea bag from the box. Unwinding the string from the tea bag, she dropped it into the empty mug before her.

Then, carefully, Sally poured in the boiling water. Her eye glanced down curiously at the saying on the paper tab attached to the tea bag, for this was her morning ritual. Yogi tea bags always seemed to have a lot to say about her life.

"*The truth is the kindest thing we can give folks in the end,*" it read. The quotation was attributed to Harriet Beecher Stowe.

Sally put the kettle back on the stove as tears welled in her eyes. The truth was, indeed, the kindest thing, especially when it came to her relationship with Frankie. She had to share her barest, most vulnerable self. Otherwise, how would Frankie ever know her…or even love her?

Just as Sally had expected, she'd heard from her guides in no uncertain terms. And they were definitely blessing the idea of telling Frankie, as if she even needed the clarification. She'd tell her lover at the right moment.

If Frankie left her, Sally had simply chosen the wrong woman. Yet again.

It was time for the truth to be revealed.

Chapter Thirteen

Monroe walked onto the church balcony and peeled off their dirty, gray particulate mask. Dropping down on to a pew, they looked out dully at the sanctuary. There were only a few dozen more boxes of moldy sheet music to sort through. Presumably, it would take the rest of the week.

The work was hard, dirty, and tiresome, and it couldn't be put off any longer. Seven black garbage bags, filled to the brim with trashed papers, were already stuffed into the church's recycling bins outside. Monroe was exhausted.

They leaned back in the pew and yawned, and at that moment spotted something moving down below in the chancel. Monroe sat forward and peered into the sanctuary below.

It was Kate. Quietly, Monroe studied her from above. Kate had barely been seen in the last few days, and Monroe watched curiously, ignoring the flutter in their gut.

Why was Kate so intensely interesting? And what was she doing down there, anyway?

Monroe studied Kate for a moment. She was looking intently at the items on the altar. Silently, she studied the set of Unitarian chalices before her, each fitted with a pillar candle. One was for general worship and prayer. The other, a red candle, was designated to honor the Black Lives Matter movement. Monroe watched as Kate traced the edges of the chalice with her fingertip.

Kate wandered away from the altar now. She walked down the center aisle and sat in a pew in the middle of the sanctuary. Leaning forward, she picked up a copy of the paperback teal hymnal where the newer UU hymns, the Pete Seeger songs, and the Holly Near protest anthems could be found.

Monroe watched Kate slowly turn a few pages, then return the book to the shelf underneath the pew in front of her. She was apparently just wandering around, trying to find something to occupy her mind.

Her movements were insignificant, yet somehow Monroe couldn't take their gaze off of her.

*

Kate sat back in her pew and stared out at nothing. It was important to get out of her small cell-like bedroom every so often; she knew that. Especially when she could barely force herself out of bed in the morning.

The problem was that Kate could no longer see the point to any of this.

Catalina had knocked on her door that morning with a fresh cup of coffee with condensed milk at half past seven. She also handed Kate a plate with a few warmed tortillas and butter. "Room service," she'd called it. Then she looked at Kate with concern.

"Come on, *flaquita*—you have to get up. You have to eat. You've got to do something today."

Kate had assured Catalina that she would do exactly that, of course. That she even had a work project to get started on. But as soon as Catalina left, Kate went straight back to bed, just as she always did these days. Sleep was becoming her best refuge.

Because here was the truth: Kate knew this day would pass like all the others so far, in a slow-motion imitation of life. She had discovered that being in sanctuary was a great sea of nothingness, even with her freelance marketing work to keep her occupied.

It would have been easy to set up her laptop in an empty classroom and set to work, to actually accomplish something. Yet still she retreated. Kate knew what was wrong, of course.

It was Lizzy.

Since their fight, she'd heard from her girlfriend repeatedly, but she hadn't once responded. Lizzy hadn't given up on her, of course. Far from it. There had been several bags of groceries left for her, each with a note encouraging her, or simply saying Lizzy was thinking about her. One bag even had a pair of fuzzy socks because Kate had complained weeks earlier that her feet were cold in the stone-clad room she slept in.

Once, Kate even started to walk into the church kitchen, not realizing Lizzy was in there, talking to Catalina. "Just tell her I said hi," she could hear Lizzy say.

Kate froze outside the kitchen door. Then she pressed her body against the wall so she was undetectable in the darkness of the corridor. Kate listened, her heart practically beating out of her chest.

The tone in Lizzy's voice was haunting. She sounded calm and resolute. And achingly sad.

Still, Kate could not get herself to reply to Lizzy's texts. It seemed impossible somehow as the reality of her life in sanctuary began to sink more deeply into her psyche. There was no getting out of this. Not now. Not ever.

It was time for someone to finally be a realist. And if that had to be her, then so be it.

Kate needed to prepare for the obvious. She would almost certainly have to go back to Ireland. And if Lizzy wouldn't come with her, then they had to break up. There simply wasn't any other choice.

This was a point reinforced by her calls to the immigration attorney who expressed neither optimism nor hope. Instead, the lawyer was all business when she bothered to answer the phone.

"I'll get back to you when there's something to report," was how she put it in her crisp, official-sounding voice.

The previous Sunday, in an effort to cope, Kate had even attended a church service. She and Catalina sat in a pew surrounded by the earnest, liberal Unitarians singing *We Shall Not Be Moved* in Spanish.

Then, as soon as it was over, Kate retreated back to her tiny bedroom prison. But before she went, she happened to glance out the window of the church sanctuary. She could see Lizzy just outside, talking to the minister. One way or another, Lizzy wasn't giving up on her. That much was obvious.

So why was she giving up…even if the facts looked grim?

Kate honestly didn't know. She just felt entirely unable to respond.

Now, there was a sound from the back of the sanctuary. A creak sounded, high up in the timbers of the church, as if someone else was there. Someone watching her. Kate turned and her eyes searched the afternoon shadows of the balcony above her.

"Hello?" she called, a little tentatively. A figure stood up in the balcony.

"Hi." It was Monroe.

Kate stood now. "Monroe! Hey…are you working?"

Monroe paused. "Yeah."

The two were silent for a moment. "I was hoping I might catch you playing again," Kate heard herself say.

Why did she just say this? Kate wasn't quite sure, but somehow it felt right.

Monroe shrugged. "I'm cleaning out the music library."

"Oh, okay."

The two continued to regard each other. "If you feel like taking a break at some point, I'd love to hear more," Kate encouraged.

What am I doing?

Monroe disappeared.

*

Monroe's heart pounded hard as they took the stairs two at a time. Meanwhile, Monroe's mind was going berserk.

Calm the fuck down. This woman has a girlfriend. She just wants to hear you play the piano.

That's all.

Still, these thoughts had no effect as Monroe hurried up the side aisle toward the old Steinway. A command performance for Kate was far preferable to facing the rest of the mildewed mess in the tower. That was for damn sure.

Monroe slowed as they approached, and Kate stood up. "Hi," she said. "Thank you. I've been in need of a good distraction."

"Me, too," Monroe murmured. "What do you want to hear?"

Kate hesitated. Asking to hear more of Monroe's original compositions seemed like a bad idea.

"Anything," Kate said. Then she seated herself in the pew directly across from the piano as Monroe straddled the bench. They smiled at each other.

"Debussy?"

"Whatever you fancy."

Monroe took a deep breath and turned toward the keys. Then touching fingers to keyboard, they played the first few quiet phrases of *La fille aux cheveux de lin*. Monroe's touch barely pressed the keys as the first delicate notes sounded, then they built to the first major chord resolution.

The piece moved on, haltingly at first. Then it picked up strength as the musical motif repeated itself. Stronger, bolder chords built now.

These chords were Kate's chords because Kate was strong, wasn't she?

At least Monroe imagined she was. Because you'd have to be strong to choose sanctuary.

Now, a single note—an F sharp—hung in the air, suspending the entire composition with it.

This was where Kate was now, hanging suspended in mid-life, waiting for the moment of her liberation, when she could walk away from sanctuary with a home in the US. Or not.

Once again the chords moved on, stately, orderly, because this was indeed the process Kate was caught in. The legal system. The church system. Both of them chafing, demanding she fall in line and be orderly.

But perhaps Kate was not the orderly type. Perhaps she was wilder. Freer than that.

Monroe hit the pedal again, softening the strike of chords as their left hand picked up its pace, and their right hand explored the upper reaches of the melody. A few minor chords and another upward arpeggio took the exploration into the final forte climax.

Monroe was playing with all of their focus and power now as soaring, impassioned chords filled the air. Here was the culmination of the piece.

This was the natural result of Kate's time in sanctuary. Emotions expressed. Passions explored.

Discoveries made.

Moments later, the piece ended, and Monroe's fingers rested on the final keys, releasing them to precious silence.

Kate paused. Then gently she began to applaud. "Extraordinary," she said. "Bravo! You are a fine pianist, Monroe." She beamed at Monroe. "What was that?"

"La fille aux cheveux de lin."

"I've never heard of it." Kate gazed at Monroe curiously. "What does it mean?"

Monroe looked down at the keys, their voice now barely audible. "The Girl with the Flaxen Hair."

Kate smiled. "Wow," she said lightly as a blush spread across Monroe's face.

Monroe scrambled to explain. "I mean, you're blonde or flaxen or whatever. Sort of. I...I don't know, I just thought you'd...you know…like it." Monroe's voice disappeared.

Kate smiled once more. "I love it. Honestly, Monroe, it's the first thing that has made me smile in days. I needed it." Her smile broadened. "Your music has a healing effect on me."

Monroe now looked up at Kate, steadfastly ignoring the incessant pounding of their heart. "I'm glad to hear it." Monroe paused for a moment, uncertain what to say next. "So…it's been rough?"

"It's been hell."

Monroe sighed, gazing at Kate. "I can totally understand."

"I'm grateful! Don't get me wrong, Monroe. If it weren't for you I wouldn't even be here," Kate continued in a rush. "But I'm rather lost if you want to know the truth."

Monroe just nodded, trying to ignore the hopeful swell in their heart.

"I suppose anyone might be a bit blue while they're in sanctuary, but it seems impossible for me to get the papers that I need to stay. At least, It's not going to happen in the next few weeks." Kate paused. "It's difficult."

Monroe nodded. "I can only imagine."

There was a pause.

Monroe stood awkwardly. "I…I guess I'll…go."

Kate looked surprised. "Oh?"

Monroe nodded toward the tower above them. "Got to get back to work."

"Right. Well, anyway, thank you." Kate began to applaud once more.

Monroe gave a stiff little bow, cheeks burning. "Thanks," they mumbled. Then turning, Monroe hurried back along the side aisle toward the stairs to the balcony.

Kate was left alone to ponder her fate, while Monroe took the stairs two at a time, lit with new possibility.

*

Sally pushed along on her beater bike, barely able to keep up with Frankie, who was tucked into a blur far ahead of her. But then Frankie was the cyclist, not her. Her bike alone was evidence of that.

It was an aging Schwinn with a lopsided basket attached to the handlebars, a smattering of rust across the frame, and three cranky speeds. She'd gotten it for free from Craigslist.

"Wait up!" Sally called, panting hard as she stood up on the pedals.

To her left, a brilliant morning was unfolding over the Bay. There was a slight chop in the water, and the sky was the palest of blues, scattered with white, vaporous streaks of cloud. Meanwhile, the Golden Gate Bridge was a tiny, orange slash on the distant horizon. To its left rose San Francisco, an urban smudge of sky-scrapers on the landscape.

Sally liked these Saturday mornings—rare as they were—with Frankie. Then they felt almost like a normal couple, not just a cop and a psychic who'd been thrust together to hash out a life together against all odds.

As she pedaled, Sally did her best not to think about the conversation she was planning to have with Frankie once they got up to the old Ford plant. Or the Craneway Pavilion as it was now officially known.

Sally pumped past strollers and joggers, avoiding the break-away pug here, the errant toddler there. On both sides of the Bay Trail, abundant reedy swamps were verdant, leading right up to the edge of the buzzing eight-lane highway just beyond them. She picked up a glimpse of a large, white egret, posed on one long, black leg among the reeds to her right.

Finally, Sally caught sight of Frankie once again, now strad-dling her bike up ahead as she rested. Frankie turned and inspected the people passing between them, and when she saw Sally's face, she visibly relaxed. Frankie gave a little wave as Sally pumped up to a stop behind her.

"Wow," Sally panted. "Guess…it's been…a while."

"You look good!"

"No, Frankie, *you* look good. Why didn't you tell me you were a cyclist?"

"You didn't ask. Anyway, who cares? We're here." Frankie pushed her sunglasses up her nose and nodded out at the Bay. "Nice day, right?"

"Incredible." It was sunny, clear, and nearly seventy. An anomaly for December.

A moment later, they set off on the last push to the Craneway. It wasn't long before it came into sight, a large, simple, old structure of brick and glass that settled in right along the Bay.

Built in the thirties, the former Ford plant became the largest automotive plant in the West. On one side were ancient railroad tracks, and on the other was the Bay and a large commercial loading dock. And it was here that hundreds, even thousands, of Jeeps and armored tanks were built, mostly by women. They were the very vehicles that helped England and the Allies win World War II.

Moments later, Frankie and Sally pulled up and stopped their bikes. Then they got off and locked them up. "Being here is kind of cool, makes me think of the Rosies," Frankie said.

"The Rosie the Riveters?" Immediately Sally thought of the emblematic poster from the forties. A cheeky brunette in a work shirt and a red, polka-dotted scarf flexes her arm beneath the headline, "We can do it!"

"Some of those old gals are still around here. They must be pushing a hundred," Frankie said. "You know, every year thousands of people show up here dressed as Rosie the Riveter. It's like a Parks thing. And damned if those original Rosies don't show up, too."

They were quiet for a moment, looking out over the water.

Sally smiled at her girlfriend. "Did you ever dress up as Rosie the Riveter?"

Frankie gave her a look. "I'm usually working, Sally. Anyway, trust me. I look terrible in polka dots."

"Are you sure?" Sally shot her girlfriend her most flirtatious smile.

"Very sure. Come on." Reaching out, Frankie took Sally's hand, and the two of them now began to walk along the dock, hand in hand.

A small tremble of fear began in Sally's gut. Still, she had to get on with it, and now was as good a time as any. Frankie seemed to be in a good mood, the sun was shining, and when was it going to get easier to make her request?

"So Frankie…honey …" Sally cleared her throat. "Being here makes me think of something," she began.

"What's that, babe?"

"Mmm, so this thing happened at work." Sally tried to keep her tone light and casual.

"Yeah? What's that?" Frankie's voice sounded mellow and relaxed.

Good. This was going as planned. So far.

"So, like I told you, I've been doing some readings at the store."

"I know. Psychic readings," Frankie said evenly.

"Right," Sally glanced at her girlfriend quickly, almost afraid at what she'd see. Still, Frankie's face betrayed no emotion. Instead, she was still gazing out at the movement on the water impassively. Sphinx-like.

"I gave this one reading," Sally continued. "I think the woman was in tech—I don't know for sure, but that was the feeling I got."

Frankie continued to study the Bay, hands in the pocket of her cycling jacket. "And?"

Sally hesitated. "Umm…well, I saw some really bad stuff. Like…a sniper. On a roof. Killing people."

Frankie remained silent.

"And I could see it was tied to social media." Sally hesitated. "And it was right here, in Jack London Square."

Frankie faced her now and looked at Sally curiously. "And you're telling me this…why?"

"Because I think someone needs to know, Frankie. Someone official."

Frankie continued to study her lover as if weighing each one of her words.

"Don't you think we should tell someone?" Sally continued. "There were dead people all over the ground in Jack London, Frankie. It looked terrible. And I could totally see this woman's company was responsible. They were supposed to be preventing something like this, but they were aiding and abetting, or whatever you call it. They were influencing people to show up there. And get killed."

Frankie sighed. "Oh, Sally," was all she said, but her face betrayed how she felt.

Sally's voice took on a note of pleading. "Come on, Frankie. You've got to help me with this. You're a cop. You're supposed to stop crimes like this."

Frankie rolled her eyes. "First of all, it's the FBI who handles that kind of thing…but seriously. Honey. No one can do anything with a psychic tip."

"Why not?"

"Because it's not real, baby. Please. You know it's not."

A look of shock passed across Sally's face. "Excuse me?"

Frankie held a hand up. Now she began to backpedal. "Wait, I mean—lookit, Sally. We disagree about the whole psychic thing, you know we do, right? So I'm probably not the best person to help you with this. I mean…I'm just not."

Frankie's very reasonable tone whizzed right past Sally now, who was still back on being told her visions were not real. Sally was now staring at the ground, her hands on her hips.

"I thought you'd at least want to hear what's been keeping me up at night," she said in a low voice.

"Well, I do but—"

"But it's not *real*. Okay, Frankie, you've said enough," said Sally tartly, as she turned away. Swiftly, she headed back to her bike.

Frankie trailed after her. "Sally! Come on! Please…"

But Frankie's entreaties had no effect. In an instant, the lock was off of Sally's bike, and she was riding away as fast as she could. Frankie scrambled to catch up. A moment later she was riding alongside Sally.

"Come on, babe!" Frankie implored, but Sally ignored her, pedaling faster to get away. Now Sally whizzed past all obstacles in her path, riding much faster than she had been before. Frankie did her best to keep up, staying close by her rear tire. "Sally —honey—wait!"

Finally, Sally came to a halt in the middle of the trail, and Frankie almost ran into her. Sally turned around with a furious look on her face. "You know, I was worried that when I told you about this you'd break up with me on the spot," she said. "Now I'm wondering why I'm even going out with you."

"Hey—Sally!" Frankie called again, but Sally was off once more, pumping fast along the Bay Trail.

Finally Frankie slowed, realizing that Sally was not going to stop or even talk to her. Sally would go back to her home, and one of their rare Saturdays together would be ruined. And all because she'd blown her lover off.

Shit.

For the first time in forever, Frankie honestly didn't know what to do.

Chapter Fourteen

Lizzy bent over her guitar, tuning it yet again in the midst of the Breakdowns' rehearsal. The band had been hard at it for more than an hour. Carla, the bass player, gave her a confused look. "You're doing that again? I thought you just tuned five minutes ago."

"Something's wrong," Lizzy muttered.

The drummer slumped against the wall behind her and stared at the ceiling. They'd gathered for one of their regular Thursday night rehearsals. And this time, it wasn't going well.

Carla shook her head. "You're off your game, girl. This is like the seventh or eighth time you've tuned in the last half hour."

"When's Tenika getting back?" the drummer asked.

"Or Kate, for that matter." Azeb, the sax player, threw a critical look in Lizzy's direction. "It's fine, Lizzy. For real."

"Yeah…just one sec." Lizzy kept fiddling with the tuning peg on her top E as she listened to its pitch once more. She glanced up at the various players arranged in a semicircle in her garage. "I'm sorry, guys. Just bear with me."

The band just looked at her. Lizzy had been lead singer and guitarist for The Breakdowns for more than five years. Through all of their gigs, their sound checks, their rehearsals, and the endless process of trying to get booked in the East Bay, she'd been their steadfast rock. Furthermore, her instrument was always in tune.

This was new and disturbing behavior.

Carla broke the silence. "Lizzy...if you need a break, just tell us. You've got a lot going on, right now."

"I don't need a break," Lizzy protested. "Okay, so Kate's in sanctuary but that's *all* that's wrong."

The band members glanced at each other dubiously. "That's actually a lot, Lizzy." Azeb said gently. "Maybe you need to take the rest of the night off."

"It's not a lot!' Lizzy snapped. Then ran her hands through her hair nervously. "I'm sorry. Believe me, this is therapy. Anyway, we need to rehearse."

The fact that they had a gig in less than forty-eight hours wasn't a concern. Lizzy would show up and play. They knew the tunes cold. They were even tight on their endings.

The band would push on as the consummate part-time pros that they were, though admittedly they could do little without their lead singer. The bigger issue was that one of them was now quietly falling apart, and she was doing it under protest.

"Ten-minute break," declared Carla, and everyone put down their instruments and wandered away.

A moment later, she came up behind Lizzy and patted her shoulder. "So what's going on, baby girl?"

Lizzy turned around with a crestfallen look on her face. She was holding her phone, regarding her texts, and suddenly tears filled her eyes. "It's...I mean, it's dumb." She pushed at the tears on her face with annoyance and stuffed the phone into the pocket of her jeans. "It's a passing thing. That's all."

Carla was unmoved. She just looked at Lizzy, demanding more information.

"Kate's not speaking to me," Lizzy finally admitted. "I don't even know why. She threw me out the other night, just after I got to the church. She won't even answer my texts."

"Did you do something?"

"Nothing! Noth—well...actually..." Lizzy sighed and looked at her feet. "There was some discussion about how she could get out of there. And you know, I could always marry her. I mean, that's a fact, Carla. We could get married, and it would solve everything."

"So, why hasn't she married you yet?"

Lizzy shook her head. "It's complicated. She's not *not* into it. She just needs time, and time is exactly what we don't have. Kate's going to have to leave the church, probably in a few more weeks, and then who knows?"

"Sounds hard."

"It is hard; it's hard as hell. I don't have any idea how to play this, I—"

Carla leveled a look at her friend. "I wasn't talking about you, Lizzy."

Lizzy looked abashed. "Oh."

"Kate's got to be losing her mind, locked up in that place."

"Basically, she's given up, Carla. She's preparing herself to go back to Ireland."

"So go with her."

"And do what with the garage? Just pull out and leave T alone with it? The garage is my life. And what about you guys? I'd have to quit the band."

Carla shook her head. "So, you get a new band. But love is love, Lizzy. And marriage is a big fucking deal. Either way, you'd better go down there and deal with it."

"I've tried. I've—"

Carla interrupted Lizzy's mounting defense. "Did you apologize, Lizzy?"

"No," she said quietly.

Carla shook her head. "Like I thought. Just be frigging honest, and quit this shit, Lizzy. The woman's got a few thoughts of her own, you feel what I'm saying? Just quit being so defensive, and tell her you're sorry. Then let her come to you, if and when she's ready."

Lizzy let out a low moan. "Okay, fine. You're right. I know I need to apologize. But I can't just wait around for her come to me, Carla. She's giving up."

A look of sympathy crossed Carla's face. "If she's giving up, then you never had her in the first place," she said gently. "Anyway, go over to the church right now and talk to her, Lizzy. We can finish without you. I'll lock up the garage when we're done. Go make your peace. That's all you can rightly do."

Lizzy sighed. She knew her friend was right. "Okay. Thanks," she said.

Then reaching over, she gave Carla a long hug.

*

Rosalind leaned over the report on her laptop and read through its final pages one more time, as a small, triumphant feeling flickered through her. She was exhausted.

It was here that she'd cataloged one thousand seven hundred forty-six bogus social media posts that had slipped through the supposedly ironclad True Wire system. Rosalind had summarized her findings in detail, pointing out exactly where the detection robotics were flawed.

She was giving Scott and the other principals four days to respond to the report, which she'd leave on their desk tonight. She figured that was just about as long as they'd need to effectively ignore her. Then, she was going to go knocking on office doors, demanding explanations, a wire concealed under her blouse.

This much she knew. Without audio and written documentation, the press would never take her claims seriously.

Leaning back in her chair, Rosalind regarded her work for a few moments and wondered at what she'd just done. It had taken every working moment of the previous ten days to go through so many posts and find what she was looking for. She'd pushed herself with caffeine and jumping jacks to get through it, slapping her own face when she started to fall asleep over her laptop at home as each night wore on.

The path fell into place remarkably clearly. Rosalind could follow the breadcrumbs without any problem.

More and more, she'd been driven by fear as much as obligation. For each one of these bogus posts, a toxic stew of extreme rhetoric designed to prey on people's worst instincts, could have incited a small or even large riot on their own. She had no idea which ones, if any, would actually lead to something. But the fact they existed at all, and were somehow being permitted in a company that claimed to root out this very thing, rubbed against every instinct in her body.

This was fraud, pure and simple. And that was just for starters.

If her parents knew what Rosalind was doing, they'd be horrified, of course. How could their Harvard graduate daughter throw away such a *great* opportunity? That's what they'd undoubtedly demand to know the minute they found out she'd intentionally sabotaged her job.

They'd be beyond furious. Just like they would be if they knew about the sexual fantasies that regularly filled her head.

Rosalind picked up the plastic cup now filled with melting ice beside her, and pulled on the straw. The slurping sound filled the silence of the space around her. The office was basically empty now. She was alone, save for Frank, the janitor who was working his way down the hall, methodically dumping trash cans into a larger bin on wheels.

Rosalind really didn't care at this point. She'd spent so many hours listening to her family trash the gays and lesbians, who even cared what her *mama* and her *baba* thought? This was simply what fifteen years of suppressed anger looked like.

It was breakthrough time, or at least that's how Rosalind was looking at it now. So much had passed through her mind since she understood the enormity of what she'd discovered, that each day now was lit with something new.

Call it a passion, perhaps, or a mission. Whatever it was, a renewed sense of purpose now saturated her life. It got Rosalind up in the morning and put her to sleep well after her usual bedtime. She was genuinely excited each day to see what would happen next, even if she was fairly scared as well.

And eventually, perhaps *mama* and *baba* would find a way to forgive her. If they didn't, she figured, she was used to being alone.

Rosalind tossed the remainder of her melting ice in the trash, and went off to use the printer, her thumb drive and her report firmly in hand.

It was time to create a paper trail.

*

Lizzy knocked on the side door of the church, first quietly, then a little more loudly.

There was no reply.

"Kate?" she called through the crack in the door. "Honey?"

The night remained still and quiet. Lizzy glanced around. Two young men were heading across the highway overpass, beers in their hands. They were the only other people on the street. Lizzy knocked a little louder. "Are you there?" she called.

There was another moment of silence. The light she'd seen shining through the crack in the door now clicked off. Kate was clearly home.

"Please open the door, honey. Come on—it's me. I've come to apologize." Lizzy knocked again, and even gave the doorknob a shake for good measure. There was no reply.

Shit.

Lizzy walked dejectedly back to her truck, opened the door, and climbed inside. Then she leaned back against the headrest and closed her eyes, uncertain what to do next. Again, there was radio silence.

Well, all right…what else can I do?

Sometimes you were just bound to lose out. Lizzy turned on the ignition and shifted the truck into gear, but still she remained in place. She couldn't quite bring herself to pull away from the curb. Not yet.

Turning off the ignition, Lizzy climbed out of the truck once more and went over to the door. "Please open the door, Kate," she implored through the crack. "Honey…please. I just want to talk. Like I said, I need to apologize."

Lizzy held her breath, waiting for a reply. "Please?" she repeated after a moment.

There was no response. A moment later, Lizzy slowly ambled off to her truck, climbed in, and drove away.

There would be no reuniting tonight.

*

Kate lay in the morning half-light of her room, staring at the vaulted, stone ceiling far above her. She could take a shower, or at least get dressed. A small rumble in her stomach betrayed her hunger. Somewhere in the kitchen was the last of the instant oatmeal Lizzy had brought her the previous week, but she made no move toward it.

There really is no reason to get up, is there?

Especially not if she could lie there and ignore what had happened the night before. Once again, her mind reviewed the depressing details in technicolor: Lizzy shaking the doorknob. Lizzy's voice pleading to be let in.

Lizzy had done little or nothing wrong beyond loving her. Yet, there she was, asking to be forgiven from the other side of a locked door, for God's sake. It was a door that Kate simply couldn't get up and open.

Once again tears sprang into her eyes. Neither Kate nor Lizzy would get out of this unscathed, that much was clear. She would punish her lover, just as she was currently punishing herself.

Mainly because it seemed the only choice.

Dimly, somewhere in Kate's mind, she was still aware that there were other options. But they felt almost artificial now. Would she have freely accepted Lizzy's offer of marriage if she hadn't been an undocumented worker about to be deported by ICE?

Would she have *truly* wanted to marry Lizzy just because of who she was and who they were together?

Perhaps she would. Up until a few weeks earlier, it had seemed more and more likely. Though Kate couldn't say for certain because, honestly, it was still just a little too soon to know. Anyway, such thoughts were an exercise in futility. She figured she was as good as gone at this point.

Needing emotional help was the furthest thing from Kate's mind right now.

A knock on her door pulled her out of her thoughts. "I brought you tea," said the warm voice on the other side. It was Catalina. "Nice and strong. Milk and honey, too."

Catalina had learned that an Irish woman like her preferred tea to coffee, and especially with milk and honey. Kate sat up and put her feet on the floor. She simply couldn't ignore such a kind gesture. Anyway, she badly needed the tea.

Kate opened the door wide and let her friend in. Catalina smiled as she entered. "It's cold in here, *flaquita!*" she murmured, putting the steaming mug down on Kate's bureau. She looked around, uncertainly.

"Here," Kate said. She climbed back under the covers and patted a spot on the edge of the bed. Then propping herself up against her pillow, she eagerly took the mug of tea in hand. "Thank you, Catalina. I really do appreciate it."

Catalina regarded her with concern. "You all right?" Reaching over she felt Kate's forehead for a fever. "You feel okay, *flaquita?*"

Kate waved away her concern. "I'm not sick, if that's what you're worried about. I'm...I don't know..." She couldn't finish her sentence.

"Oh, my," said Catalina.

"The truth is that I'm in misery. This is a total, extreme shit show. That's how I am." Kate shook her head woefully. "Lizzy was back last night, just trying to talk to me through the door. I couldn't even let her in."

Catalina nodded. "We all do this, *flaquita*. Every last one of us who's ever been locked up in a church. It's not living. It's hiding."

Kate took a sip of the mug of tea that warmed her hands. "Exactly."

"Sometimes you want to die because it all seems so impossible, right?"

"Yes. That, too."

"You're like an animal…trapped, right?"

Kate nodded in agreement. "Right."

Catalina regarded Kate. "There's just one big difference between us, *flaquita*."

Kate took another sip of tea. "What's that?"

"You are in love, and I am not. You have someone who follows your every move…someone who misses you at night. Someone who comes around here, worrying about you so much. Me?" Catalina shrugged. "Not so lucky."

"Yes, but—"

"But nothing, *flaquita*. If there is one thing I've learned in this place, it's not to take one damn thing for granted."

Kate sipped her tea and looked at Catalina skeptically. "What?" Catalina asked.

"Nothing, I just…it's complicated."

Catalina's voice took on a gentle sing song. "It's just not that complicated, *flaquita*."

"Catalina, with all due respect—" Kate started to say but Catalina cut her off.

"You got someone who cares about you, you got to hang on

to that with all your heart, *flaquita*." Catalina leaned in toward Kate and eyed her intensely. "You don't send that person away like some dog who doesn't deserve to come in. You open the door, and you make a place in your heart. And you trust that person to love you and give you what you need. And you thank God and all those angels for bringing that person to you in the first place." She paused and looked at Kate. "Instead, you are hurting yourself. Why?"

Kate sighed and regarded the half empty mug of tea in her hands. "I know," she said softly. Every time she refused to talk to Lizzy it made her feel worse than before. "But here's the thing, Catalina. I can't offer Lizzy anything. I mean…okay. I could marry her—but what if I couldn't stay married to her? What if it didn't work out?"

"Then you get divorced, *flaquita*. It happens every ten minutes in this country. It's not the worst thing to happen, because at least you tried. At least you gave it a shot. Then you know the rest of the story…" She paused. "Otherwise, you're lost. You just go home to your other country, and it's all over. And you never know what would have happened if you'd said 'yes.'"

She gazed at Kate. "Is that really what you want?"

Kate sniffed hard as tears erupted and began to pour down her face. "No," she managed to say before shaking sobs overtook her. Catalina held out her arms and took Kate in for a long, comforting hug. "*Tranquila flaquita,*" she said. "We have a saying—*Dios aprieta pero no ahorca.* God may press you tight, but He will not shock you. You're gonna be okay."

Kate was dissolving, one piece at a time, here at the Oakland Unitarian Center for Peace and Justice. She just didn't realize the peace they were talking about was her inner peace, and the justice had something to do with the beating of her own heart. And Lizzy's.

Kate cried in earnest into Catalina's shoulder for a long time. Finally, she pulled back and looked at her friend as she wiped the tears from her face. "So what are you saying?"

"She wants to marry you, so why not? You love her, right?"

Kate nodded. "I do."

"Then marry Lizzy and get out of here, *flaquita*. You're thinking too much. Me—I wish I was that lucky. I got no one."

"But you must, Catalina. Everybody does."

Catalina gave a chuckle. "I used to have a husband, but I dumped him back in Tijuana. So now there's no one, but it's okay. I got this place. These people are good to me, and I have my eighty-three-year-old mother in Rosarito," she said. "But you, *flaquita*...you have to get out of here. You are not doing so good."

Kate took a long, shaky breath. She could see what her friend was saying. All of it was true. But somehow the slow-burning fear still had her.

"At least talk to her," urged Catalina.

Kate looked over at this warm woman with the big, brown arms who was so honest, so real. So strong. "Okay," she said finally. "Okay, I'll call Lizzy." Kate took another shaky breath and smiled at her friend. "And Catalina...thank you."

"No, thank you, *flaquita*." Catalina's silvery laugh split the air. "You give me something to worry about!"

Kate smiled and drained her tea.

Catalina was, as usual, absolutely right.

Chapter Fifteen

Frankie cruised slowly along Grand Avenue as Lake Merritt shimmered to her left. It was just another sunny day in so-called Paradise, but not for Frankie. She had things on her mind.

Desire's Magical Garden was just up ahead on the right, which probably meant Sally was there as well. Frankie pulled to a stop at the light and idled. She was done with her shift at work, and now it was time to kill the rest of the afternoon spent not seeing Sally. She supposed she could go to a movie. Or maybe walk around the lake.

Unless, of course, she could get herself to go into the store where Sally worked, ostensibly just to look around. Frankie would hate it, of course, if some estranged girlfriend showed up when she was supposed to be working, say, a public event. But then, Sally worked in a crystal shop. And that, to Frankie, seemed a different thing for sure.

Frankie still had her body armor on under her street clothes, and it itched and chafed against her skin. There hadn't been a convenient place to take it off so far today. And there still wasn't. There would almost certainly be no stepping into the back room at Sally's shop to change. Not with the way they'd left things.

Sally still wasn't returning her calls or texts. It had been three days, and Frankie was fairly bewildered. She hadn't been in this exact place with one of her lovers in…well, ever maybe?

Frankie felt not only rebuked, but totally muddled. She had no clear idea of what to do next. The light changed, and she started up again slowly. A moment later, she cruised past the magic store and glanced at it as she drove by.

The store, of course, was open. Immediately, her therapist's words of advice popped into her head. *Accepting what makes you different is just part of love.*

Part of that acceptance meant meeting her girlfriend at Ground Zero, right? Going straight into the belly of the beast, and making an informed assessment. After all, when had she ever stepped foot in a place like Desire's Magical Garden?

Exactly never.

Slowing for a moment, Frankie assessed the parking situation. No places along the street were open. The car behind her honked, and Frankie moved along once more, her mind whirring as she glanced at the retreating store in the side mirror. Sally was almost certainly in there. Frankie felt her heart beat a little faster.

Pulling up a side street, she made a quick three-point turn and began to search for parking spots on the other side of Grand. There had to be one here somewhere. But parking in this neighborhood was as tight as ever. Frankie searched up one block and down the next, and still nothing appeared.

Finally, she pulled up and parked in front of a hydrant. Getting a ticket would be humiliating, but it would ultimately be worth it.

It was time to find out what the hell was going on.

*

The chimes on Desire's door tinkled as Frankie let herself in. She glanced around, hands on hips as the smell of sandalwood incense hit her full force. Immediately, her eye scanned the counter, looking for Sally.

A tall woman with silver hair cascading past her shoulders

was behind the counter. She was ringing up a purchase for a young woman. There was no sign of Sally.

Assuming a casual air, Frankie began to wander through the store, looking at things. Goddess statues, cases of crystals, and esoteric books swam in front of her as she took one deep breath and then another. She tried to calm her wildly beating heart, just as she tried not to notice an entire display of pillar candles invoking things like Animal Communication and Instant Prosperity.

Frankie was a fish out of water and she knew it. Her eye now caught a small bottle on a shelf full of bottles. 'Protection' it said on its brown paper label.

Jesus, she thought miserably. This was worse than she thought.

Frankie stepped up to the counter and the silver-haired woman gazed at her pleasantly. "May I help you?"

"I was wondering if…uh…Sally is here?"

The woman smiled. "It's Sally's day off. Were you hoping for a reading?"

"No—I," Frankie faltered. Then she stopped herself. There was no need to run away. She could be here. In fact, in a strange way, she wanted to be here. Somehow it made her feel closer to Sally.

Frankie took in the woman across from her. Clearly, she was the owner of the place. "Are you Desire?"

"Mmm-hmm. And you are…?"

"I'm Frankie." Frankie extended her hand and the woman took it. Her handshake was limp and cool. "Welcome," she said.

Then she just waited. The two women eyed each other.

Frankie shifted uncomfortably. "How much is a reading?" she finally heard herself ask.

"Depends on how long you'd like one. Thirty minutes…sixty minutes, perhaps? My assistant will be back shortly. Then I'd be happy to give you one myself."

Frankie said nothing. She felt paralyzed. Perhaps Sally had told Desire all about her. On the other hand, maybe she hadn't said a word.

Desire's blue-eyed gaze didn't leave Frankie's face. "Is there something on your mind you'd like clarity around?"

Once again, the therapist sounded in Frankie's head. *Accepting what makes you different is just part of love.*

"No…well, I guess," Frankie said reluctantly. "I mean, sort of."

"You're a newbie, huh?"

Frankie swallowed and nodded.

"Good for you for coming in. This isn't for everyone." Desire waved toward the content of the store. Then her eyes returned to Frankie. "But some people find answers here."

"I'm not looking for answers, actually. I—" Frankie began, but then she stopped. Maybe just once she could watch and learn.

Just this once.

For Sally.

"I'll take a sixty-minute reading," Frankie said, reaching for the wallet in her back pocket.

"Perfect." The woman began to ring her up. Just then the door opened, as a young trans man entered. "Ah…good timing. Hal's just back from his break. We can begin in just a moment."

"Okay," said Frankie, turning back to the store after she retrieved her credit card. *What in God's name am I doing?* She had no idea, but somehow it felt right. She wandered over to the three-figured statue of a sword-bearing goddess in the corner.

"That's Hecate," Desire said behind her. "In Ancient Greece she was seen as the protector of the households. Have you heard of Persephone?"

Frankie nodded dumbly. She actually hadn't, but at this moment it seemed better to fit in than to ask a lot of questions.

Desire continued on. "Hecate helped Persephone find her mother again by flying her through the underworld with flaming torches. It is said she wore a headdress of stars."

Frankie studied the statue. Somehow she was mesmerized

by the ornate hunk of wood. "So she was a warrior, this Hecate?"

Desire joined her now at the altar. "In an entirely feminine way, yes. These days Hecate is shown in triple form because she could stand at a crossroads, looking in all directions. The poet Sappho called her 'the most shining one.'"

"Sappho, the lesbian love poet?"

Desire smiled at Frankie. "Mm-hmm." It struck Frankie now that Desire knew exactly who she was. On the other hand, maybe just about everyone was a lesbian in a magic store in the East Bay.

Frankie looked around, hands still on hips, trying to get her bearings.

"Come this way," said Desire, advancing on a small room near the back. She pulled back the heavy curtains over the doorway and motioned Frankie inside.

It was time to get on with her reading.

*

Ten minutes later, Frankie stared at the array of cards on the small, round table. They made absolutely no sense to her, but Desire pored over them with focused intent.

"There's some kind of break up going on. But it's possible it's not permanent. Really, it's up to you," she said. "I'd call it a bump in the road, because you could have a great path with this person. If you wanted it." Desire was silent for a moment. "You love her," she said slowly. Then she looked at Frankie.

"Is that a problem?" she asked Frankie.

"What? No—I…" Frankie realized she had no idea how to reply.

Was it a problem?

"Do you know who I am?" Frankie finally asked. It felt like time to get to the point.

"Of course I do. I just ran your Master Card. You're Francesca Kennedy," Desire said, turning her blue-eyed gaze to Frankie.

"Other than that, dear, you're just another reading." She returned her focus to the cards in front of her.

Frankie studied the woman, trying to glean what was just below the surface. She totally should have checked this place out before she came in here.

"And if you were to ask me, I'd say you're rather apprehensive," Desire continued, eyes still on the cards. "And that's fine. Many of us are risk-averse."

Frankie swallowed and glanced around uncertainly. There was no place to go but forward. "Please continue."

She needn't have said it, though, for Desire was already turning more cards over and gleaning more truths. "Health is fine. Work is fine, if a bit tedious at times. It looks like it involves a lot of waiting around."

That was certainly true enough.

"And this man you work for. He can be rather…how shall I say it? Unsympathetic? Really the big issues at work are past scars." Desire looked up at Frankie. "Are you in the military, perhaps?"

"No," Frankie sighed. "I mean, I was a long time ago, but not now. Not exactly."

"But there is some violence-based trauma here." Desire's voice slowed and she closed her eyes. "A child has joined us. She is saying you're the only one who understands. And she is thanking you." An involuntary shiver ran down Frankie's spine, and she shifted in her seat uncomfortably.

"A child?" she managed to squeak.

"A girl. A girl who died."

Suddenly, tears sprang into Frankie's eyes and she could feel her heart squeeze shut. "Please—no more—" she started to say, but instead Desire took her hand.

"She says you're very, very brave," she said. "Like Hecate. But that is why you, in particular, have been given this work. Just trust it."

"My career work?"

"All of it," Desire said, studying the cards. "Your job. Love. Relationships. It's all connected, and it's all work, Frankie. The little girl is showing me there is one place where you still need to be brave." She looked up. "Does that make sense?"

Frankie shook her head slowly. She couldn't quite fathom what was happening. Sally had to have tipped her off. But Sally would never guess Frankie would actually come in the shop, let alone have a reading from her boss. Frankie's mind sputtered and whirred.

Maybe Desire had seen one of the few photos she'd allowed Sally to take of her. Somehow this, too, seemed unlikely.

"Do you have any specific questions?" Desire now asked.

"Well, I guess. My…friend wants me to do something for her. Something that is professionally very difficult for me."

"Okay," Desire said lightly, picking up the cards and shuffling them. She offered the deck to Frankie after a moment. "Pick three."

Frankie chose three cards and laid them on the table. Desire turned over the first one. "This is what happened in the past. I get a sense of isolation. Aloneness. Yet, here, in the second card, there is turmoil. Here's where you are becoming loosened up. It's always a good sign. Turn over the third card."

Frankie picked up the card and laid it on the table. It was the Queen of Swords.

"Well, of course! The Queen of Swords is like the wise elder, and she signals transformation. For her warrior has a softer side. She's not just the tough guy in the room. She's more grounded, more willing. More open."

"More open," Frankie intoned.

"Does that answer your question?"

"I think so," Frankie said, then she leaned back and exhaled. She gazed at the cards. They had been remarkably accurate, and oddly reassuring.

More open. What other message should she have expected from a psychic reading?

Frankie stood up now, and reached for her backpack. "Thanks, Desire."

"How did you hear about Sally?" Desire asked as she gathered up the cards once more.

Frankie paused. It would be so very easy to lie at such a moment, but that, too, seemed wrong. "I know her. I'm actually her girlfriend."

Desire laughed out loud. "Really? Oh, that is great. Just great!"

"Is it?"

"Well, of course. Who better to be on a learning path with than Sally? That woman is a dear old soul and a gifted reader. I'd say you chose very well." Desire rapped the cards on the table to straighten them up. Then she slid them into their box and closed the lid. "Come back anytime, Frankie. I'd be happy to read for you."

But Frankie barely heard her. She was too busy hurrying toward the door. She had to talk to Sally.

Now.

*

Monroe stirred a teaspoon of sugar into their tea, and then another. They weren't a big fan of tea, but it seemed important to embrace all things Kate at this point. And Kate drank tea.

After the tea steeped the requisite two minutes, Monroe took one sip of the Irish Breakfast blend and then another. It was smoky, slightly dark, and a little bitter, even with sugar. It was nowhere near as delicious as a freshly made Americano straight up. But then, these were the little things you did for love.

Sitting at the kitchen table, Monroe gazed out at two hummingbirds cavorting on the naked branches of a nearby tree. How they all got along in the winter was a mystery, even with the warm, sunny weather they'd been having lately. Because at any moment, all hell could break loose with another atmospheric river. Or worse.

Weather wise, these were end times in the Bay Area. If it wasn't the floods, the mudslides, and the earthquakes, it was the wildfires that were bound to bring you down.

Idly, Monroe watched the two hummingbirds at play. One buzzed the other, then together they flitted furiously, suspended in mid-air together, beaks touching, before taking off at high speed in opposite directions.

It was a sign, Monroe decided. A sign from God that something actually might happen with Kate. Lizzy hadn't appeared at all in recent days, though it was possible she might visit at night when Monroe was usually gone. Monroe would have to ask Catalina about this.

For if one thing was sure, Kate made Monroe's heart beat just a bit faster, and their blood run a little quicker. And Kate had seemed so forlorn lately. Perhaps all she needed was love. Real love. That would be the committed, dedicated, pure-from-the-heart kind a sensitive soul like Monroe could deliver.

When they closed their eyes, they saw Kate. And when they opened them, they saw her as well. A hundred times a day, Monroe wondered where Kate might be, or what she might be doing. Since Kate was always within the confines of the church, it wasn't hard to imagine.

This was just the way Monroe liked it.

Perhaps it was finally time for Monroe to say something. The speech wouldn't be oppressive or even flirtatious. It would just be vulnerable, honest, and real. And it would have music. Specifically, the unfinished piece, which was now well on the way to being finished. It was the one Monroe had played for Kate that very first time in the sanctuary.

Monroe rose, mug of tea in hand. It was time to get back to the keyboard and the unfinished composition.

And yes, they'd better check in with Catalina as well.

*

Kate stepped into the narrow stall shower and let the steaming water pour over her. Catalina was right, of course. That's pretty much all she'd been able to think about all morning since their talk.

And yet...

Somehow she still hadn't picked up the phone and called Lizzy. It was her damnable fear again, the same fear that always seemed to intrude at times like this. Kate opened the bottle of body wash and put a liberal squirt in her hand. The scent of tea tree and eucalyptus filled the air. Usually it lightened her mind, but not at the moment.

She was too preoccupied. Spreading the shower gel across her naked body, Kate let the hot shower soothe her and spray away her tension, however briefly.

If she called Lizzy and let her back into her life, wouldn't the ending—if and when it came—be all the more impossible to bear? Wasn't it truly better to just cut and run now while she still could?

Yes, she'd been convinced Catalina was right only hours earlier. But now, in the cold, hard light of day, a new reality dawned. The unfairness of expecting Lizzy to bail her out, and the pressure it would put on both of them to marry before they were truly ready, was a risk just too great to take.

Wasn't it?

Now Kate opened the bottle of shampoo on the windowsill above her, and put some in her hand. A slight aroma of rosemary drifted down as she shampooed her wet hair.

After all, Catalina was just another romantic, another cheerleader on Team Love, rooting for happy endings all around. Naturally she would insist that Kate run full throttle toward marriage instead of away from it. But marriage was seriously permanent. It was for life. Wasn't that equally important?

Back and forth Kate went, weighing each option as she'd done for the last several hours. There was no easy solution, that was for sure.

A few moments later, she got out of the shower and dried herself off. She knew she needed to call Lizzy…but not just yet. There would be a right time and place, and she would wait for that awareness to descend on her.

Until then, it was strictly wait and see. No matter what Catalina thought.

*

"I'm glad you made time for me," Rosalind's boss began. Scott motioned for Rosalind to join him at the window. "Want a kombucha?"

"No, I'm good."

She eyed her boss out of the corner of her eye. He stood transfixed, as usual, staring out at the comings and goings of boats and ships on Oakland's Inner Harbor.

"So, Rosalind…" he began.

Rosalind swallowed. It had been several days since she'd delivered her analysis to his desk, and her nerves were on edge. She fully expected to be fired for insubordination, or whatever he considered her report to be. On the other hand, he could be pleased.

Rosalind truly had no idea what to expect. She took a deep breath, trying to calm her jangled nervous system.

A heavy arm came around her shoulder. "I've got to hand it to you," Scott began, smiling at her warmly.

"You do?" Rosalind swallowed, inching out of his embrace.

"That report, first of all, was brilliant. And thorough. You really saw the whole thing, Ros. All of it in one big, beautiful piece." Scott nodded happily out the window, hands now tucked into the pockets of his high-end gray hoodie. As usual, he was dressed up for work like a Zuckerberg clone.

Rosalind remained silent, waiting for the other shoe to drop.

"Yup," he continued. "You didn't leave one stone unturned."

He fairly sang the word 'stone' as his face lit up. Now Scott folded his arms and tucked his hands up under his armpits. "You're probably the first analyst we've had who got it all figured out within... what...a month or two? Nice work, Ros."

"Rosalind."

"Yeah. So here's why this is so important." Scott glanced at her. "You want to be in on this, Ros. I promise you."

She did her best to give her boss an uncomprehending look. "Sorry?"

Scott laughed as he looked at her. "Oh, come on, Ros. You know what I'm talking about."

"No?" *Here it comes,* she thought with satisfaction as she did her best to look confused.

He took a step toward her. "The robotic misfires," he said in a low voice. "They're all set up."

Pay dirt!

"I'm sorry, I don't understand," she bluffed, milking the moment. But now Scott didn't quite buy it.

"Smart girl like you? Really?" he asked skeptically. Scott glanced around uncomfortably, before he focused on Rosalind again. She looked at him with what she hoped was an expression of pure, melting innocence.

"All right," he sighed. "All right. Usually I don't have to break this down, but if I must, I must. The flaws in our system are never going away..." Scott looked at her intently. "Do you get what I mean?"

Rosalind just continued to look at him.

Scott sighed at her apparent lack of comprehension. "The truth is they're extremely valuable."

Rosalind opened her eyes slightly in mock surprise. "I don't get it. To who?"

Now Scott threw up his arms and laughed at her. "Seriously, Ros? Wake up, honey." Once more he lowered his voice. "Those big, shiny social media platforms aren't our only clients."

Rosalind swallowed. "Oh," she said in a small voice.

"Like I said, the misfires are all hacked into the system. Because there are people out there who would…you know…benefit." Scott leaned back and looked at her, a smug smile spreading across his face. "Anyway, you can have a piece of it, too, honey. But only if you promise to keep your mouth shut."

Rosalind cocked her head. "How big a piece?"

"What—now you want to negotiate?" Scott laughed out loud. "You're a hard one to figure, Ros."

Again she gave no reply. She just looked at him with a tepid smile on her face.

Scott took a step back. "Well, this wasn't in the script, that's for damn sure." He glanced at his pink Apple watch, which had begun to ping, signaling his next meeting. "Let's just say there are other players. Big players."

"Like what…foreign government kind of players?"

"That's all I'm saying for now, Ros. Are you in or are you out?"

Now she smiled sweetly. "I can't really say until I have more details, Scott. Who's involved, how much are you paying me? That kind of thing…"

He threw up his hands. "Jesus! Okay—fine. Fifteen thousand a month. The report has already been wiped off of our servers and all paper copies destroyed. But you've got to give me your originals and all paper copies before the first check is delivered. And all supporting research."

"Really? Only fifteen thousand for that? You say it's so valuable…"

"Christ! Twenty thousand. But that's it." Now Scott looked mildly disgusted.

She looked at him boldly. "And who are we doing business with exactly?"

Distastefully, Scott pursed his lips. "What are you on, like some…crusade here, Ros?"

Rosalind didn't move a muscle. She just waited for him to relent. Finally, he couldn't stand it anymore.

"Why do you want to know this?" he asked, studying her intently.

Rosalind shrugged as she felt heat spread up through her chest. She had to be careful here. Scott was becoming suspicious.

"I just do. I like to know what I'm committing to," she said. Then she smiled. "It all sounds incredibly interesting. So, you know…I want to know more."

"Well, how about we suffice to say there are other actors here. And I'm not at liberty to say who," he replied steadily. Scott returned his gaze to the scene beyond the windows. "Are you in or are you out?"

"I mean, Scott…" she began. "If you played this right, you could even bring in foreign governments. The Russians would probably kill for a piece of this."

Now Scott shot her a dazzling smile. "Bingo," he said.

Bingo indeed.

Scott turned his full attention to her now. "So?"

Rosalind did her best to give him a cocky smile. "Maybe for twenty-five thousand a month. Let me think about it overnight."

She started to turn away, but he grabbed her wrist. "Rosalind—you're not leaving the building. And the twenty-five is fine, but you have to commit right now." Suddenly his tone turned cold, as if a switch had been turned. "You'll also need to give me everything you have." Scott's voice returned back to its usual hon-eyed tone. "Then…hey … it's bounty time."

"All right, Scott. No problem. I'm in," she said easily. Then she held up the wrist he was still gripping. "But you're going to have let go of me."

Slowly, he released her wrist. "I expect you back in here with those papers in the next three minutes." Scott turned to his watch and set the timer with a flourish. "Starting now."

Rosalind turned and hurried toward the door. "That's three hundred thousand a year, Ros," he said behind her. "And all your work is already done."

Moving fast, Rosalind hurried down the hall. But instead of going to her office, she walked straight to the emergency staircase. Slipping inside, she began barreling down the seven flights to the street.

In an instant, she hit the midday sunshine and took off in a sprint. Rosalind ran across one street and then the next, working her way through the lunchtime crowd near Jack London Square. Rounding the corner, she sprinted down the steps of the garage toward her waiting car. And as she did, she reached inside her bra and turned off the tiny wire that had been recording their conversation.

Suddenly, Rosalind felt entirely, totally free. Possibly for the first time in her life.

It was good to be alive.

Chapter Sixteen

The attorney looked over the paperwork spread out on the desk before her. Then she tapped a pen against her chin as she considered the question at hand.

"How many years did Katherine work illegally?" she asked without looking up.

"It's Kate. Seven. I think." Lizzy felt entirely awkward standing in for Kate in her meeting with the immigration lawyer she'd just hired. But then, the entire situation was awkward—including the fact that Kate most certainly wouldn't reply to any questions Lizzy might text her.

She only hoped Kate still wanted legal status in the US. Because Lizzy was applying for her, regardless.

"Seven years. Hmmm," murmured the attorney. She pondered an invisible spot in front of her, and considered her options. "That's not the *worst* thing in the world," she began slowly. "And she has no criminal charges of any kind?"

"Definitely not."

"Will your combined incomes be more than twenty-one thousand, one hundred and thirty-seven per year?"

"Yes."

"And you're comfortable signing an Affidavit of Support saying you'll support her financially?"

Lizzy smiled. "Yes, of course."

The attorney closed the folder and folded her hands. She trained a focused gaze at Lizzy.

"Okay," she said. "Here's what you can do. Marry Kate as soon as you can in the church where she's in sanctuary. But don't let her leave the building under any circumstances. At that point she'll only have immediate relative status, but she'll still be protected from an ICE bust. Kate's going to have to stay at the church for another eight to ten months max while a conditional green card gets processed for her."

Lizzy let out a cry of defeat. "Eight to ten months! Whoa whoa whoa—"

"I know it seems like a long time, Lizzy, but hear me out. At that point Katherine—Kate—*can* leave the church. Then it will be another fourteen months or so before you both have to show up for the marriage interview. That's where USCIS tries to figure out if you're actually a legit couple. And clearly you are, so they should grant her status and a green card no problem."

Lizzy squirmed in her chair. "It's not that I'm impatient. We'll wait as long as it takes. The problem is the church. She's not there legally, like the other sanctuary person is. They don't have enough showers or permits or something, so she'll have to leave soon."

"You're just going to have to plead your case to the minister, Lizzy. Explain the circumstances. Maybe she'll make an exception. It's that or find another church."

"And there are no others…" Lizzy said dubiously. All hope was quickly draining away, simply because of available space. She stood up and picked her backpack off the floor, unsure what to do next. If there even was anything that could be done.

"Well, thanks… I mean, I appreciate you reviewing the case and all."

The attorney leaned forward over her desk. "Lizzy, you got Kate into sanctuary. That's the hardest part. You can make this work. Just start talking to people."

Lizzy stuck her hands in her pockets as anxiety descended. She looked intently at the attorney. "Kate can't get deported," she said, a note of pleading in her voice. "She just can't."

"Then go make something happen," the attorney said calmly. "You can do it."

"Yeah. Maybe." Then again, maybe she couldn't.

A moment later, Lizzy stepped into the elevator and rode from the eleventh floor down to the street. Now her thoughts turned to Tenika.

At this point, Lizzy felt just plain weary. Especially because she still didn't know where Kate stood about any of this. But Tenika would know what to do, just like she always did. Which is how she'd earned the nickname 'The Fixer.' Tenika knew exactly what buttons to push and which levers to pull.

Briefly Lizzy considered calling her friend once more in the middle of nowhere. And immediately, she dismissed it. *Poor Delilah and T only had a few days left to their honeymoon. Let them enjoy it in peace.*

Anyway, once Tenika heard that Lizzie was once again rushing Kate to get married, her personal brand of hell was most definitely going to be unleashed. She could hear it now.

Girl, you just can't listen to reason...

What the hell was she supposed to do now?

*

Frankie paused before Sally's door. She peered at her reflection in the plate glass window beside her and tried to check how she looked, but there was a glare. She ran a quick hand across her matted curls anyway, hoping for the best. Then Frankie rang the doorbell.

There was silence.

The day of her psychic reading, Frankie had rushed straight over to this very same door. She'd stood outside, waiting patiently for a long time after no one answered. She'd waited mainly because part of her fully expected Sally to eventually emerge, invite her in, and forgive her.

Part of her also just wanted to linger, not quite ready to leave. Even when it was obvious Sally wasn't coming to the door.

Still a third part of Frankie's psyche actively debated whether she should leave Sally a note. The only paper she had was from work. Frankie sincerely doubted she could write a heartfelt apology on the back of an SFPD expense report. Not if she wanted it to have the right effect.

On the other hand, Frankie couldn't exactly go driving off at that moment, trying to find a card shop so she could buy some frilly piece of stationery. That seemed totally lame. Because what if Sally actually *was* at home, watching through the window and somehow testing Frankie?

What if she wanted to see how sincere Frankie was about her apology? What if Sally needed to see some kind of active demonstration of Frankie's devotion to her? Then sticking around and patiently waiting outside would be the right thing to do.

By the same token, what if Frankie returned, nicely written apology in hand, and rang Sally's doorbell again, twice in the same afternoon? Wouldn't that be just a little too stalker-esque?

On that first afternoon, Frankie was truly conflicted. After a good thirty minutes, she finally walked away, vowing to design a foolproof plan that would bring Sally back.

Now, just two days later, Frankie had returned, appropriately written note at the ready. She glanced at the lavender envelope in her right hand. She hoped to God it had the right tone and feel.

Love letters were definitely not her specialty.

Several minutes ticked by. Frankie considered whether to ring the bell once more, just for effect. But then she quieted herself and waited, using every ounce of her steely reserve to stay cool.

Get a fucking grip, she warned herself. Sally had every right to dis her once again. And yeah, okay. Fine. Sally probably wasn't home. She wasn't the type to refuse to answer the door...right? Maybe she was even at work. In which case, Frankie would leave her love note in a prominent place, maybe tucked into the door or propped against the door handle. Or better yet, slipped through the mail slot.

Sally would see it when she got home. Curious, she would bend over and pick it up. Then she would read it. Perhaps her heart might even beat a little faster when she realized it was from Frankie. Sally would certainly choose to respond at some point. She had to...didn't she?

Judging from Sally's radio silence to every one of Frankie's texts since their fight, this was not an encouraging train of thought. Frankie even briefly wondered if Sally had her phone number changed, or had even blocked her number by now.

In any case, something was off. Sally was usually a compassionate person. She wouldn't just dump Frankie in the middle of a bike ride, pedal off, and refuse to ever speak to her again. Unless, of course, she was just that furious. Frankie knew from her work that even supposedly kind people were capable of red-hot rage.

Frankie sat down on the stoop now, and gazed out at nothing in particular. What the hell was wrong with her, anyway? She'd blown it big time, and now she was being required to face the music. That's all this was. She could handle it. She just had to calm down and be patient.

Frankie took a deep breath and tried to still the pounding in her chest.

This was probably just what she needed to finally wake up and get with the program. At any rate, something had to happen. Mainly because Frankie couldn't stand the idea that her mistake had ended the relationship.

There was a creak behind her, and Frankie spun around, half-expecting to see Sally. But it was just the wind, pushing at the loose banister. Frankie stood up and set her jaw. She might as well accept it. Sally was either not home, or she wasn't answering the door for her.

Frankie slowly opened the mail slot and slipped her envelope inside. She could hear it drop softly to the floor on the other side.

She hoped to God the letter worked. It had taken her two days, several glasses of wine, and a thesaurus to get through it. It was the first love note Frankie had ever written, and for the first thirty-six hours she had no idea what to write. Finally, she Googled *How to Write a Love Letter* and some simple instructions popped right up:

Take your time and don't rush.

Use your own voice to express how you feel

Keep your partner in mind as you write the letter, as well as the level of the relationship

Remember to state your love somewhere in the letter

That much she thought she could handle. However, point three proved to be a bitch. Frankie had no idea what the 'level of the relationship' actually was…and herein lay the problem. Sally seemed committed, but was she for real?

As to point four, would it alienate Sally if Frankie came right out and declared her love? Were they honestly both ready for it?

Was Frankie?

In a word, yes. The past few days had proved remarkably instructive to Frankie. For one thing, she hadn't been able to sleep. All night long, each night, she'd grabbed her phone each time she'd woken up to see if Sally had texted. Because you never knew. Maybe Sally couldn't sleep as well.

She thought back to the torturous process of writing the letter. "…*the thought I hurt you has pushed me to a cold, sad, lonely place I never want to visit again. Please accept my apology,*" she wrote. Frankie had paused and regarded the small sea of crumpled balls of yellow paper around her, and noted that she really did feel the depths of that cold, sad lonely place. Which was some sort of progress. That's when she drained the rest of her glass of wine before she screwed up her guts and finished the letter.

If her big, romantic finish didn't do it, well, then, Frankie gave up. Because after this, she was out of ideas.

Never in her life had Frankie felt so vulnerable, so blatantly scared. Not even in the seven active shoot-outs she'd been in, or the time a perp started pummeling her on the sidewalk right in the middle of the Embarcadero. Frankie had looked up from the sidewalk and wiped the blood off of her eye to see three tourists shooting her with their iPhones.

Somehow writing Sally this love letter was a far bigger deal even than that.

Frankie stood up and slowly walked down the steps. There was nothing more to do but go home and wait for Sally's reply.

If there was one.

*

From behind one of the living room curtains, Sally watched Frankie slowly make her way down her front steps, and she felt a tug of remorse. She was not good at subterfuge. Not good at all.

But, Sally knew in this moment that silence was power. And, for once, she wanted to be the one with the power. So often, she'd been nice, cooperative, and quick to forgive. She'd made so many concessions in the past, she could practically feel the footprints of her retreating lovers on her back.

Sally was tired of being the peacemaker. For this much was clear. Frankie had disrespected her. She'd rolled her eyes just one too many times when Sally was discussing her work. If they had any chance at all, Sally would have to put herself first. She would have to turn her natural empathy down to low, and focus on what she needed for once.

And perhaps she needed to not be with Frankie at all.

Mostly what Sally needed right now was space. She needed to think through this relationship. And to be sure that Frankie was worthy of her time, her energy. Her love.

There was no denying that they had chemistry, but here's where things got confusing for Sally. Was the weak feeling she got in the pit of her stomach when she saw Frankie simply because of lust? Or was it because they were truly meant to be together?

Sally closed her eyes and let a wave of sadness engulf her. She was no longer willing to be with someone who disregarded her work—the very work she'd struggled to own for all these years. After all, it wasn't like she was a prostitute or a bookie.

She was a professional psychic, and she was proud of that fact. If her lover couldn't accept it, then perhaps that lover needed to go right back where she came from. Slowly, Sally meandered over to the door and regarded the lavender envelope now lying on the floor in front of her.

Frankie had written her a note.

Picking it up, Sally stuck it on a small table crowded with flowerpots full of Delilah's violets. Then she walked away. She'd see what Frankie had to say eventually.

But not until she was damn good and ready.

*

"Ndidi?" Rosalind stood up and extended her hand to the woman moving toward her. "I'm Rosalind."

"I'm sorry I'm late. I came as fast as I could. BART was... well, BART." The *Chronicle* reporter had an African accent, and she smiled broadly at Rosalind. There was a noticeable gap between her teeth, which was immediately disarming.

Ndidi exuded warmth, and Rosalind was grateful for it. For the past twenty-five minutes, she'd been sitting on a park bench, waiting for the reporter and worrying.

"No worries," Rosalind reassured her. "You made it out from

the city. I'm impressed."

"I checked you out. You're legit," Ndidi remarked. "Shall we walk?"

The two women began a slow stroll around Lafayette Reservoir. The tree-filled park with its rolling hills, and its walking trail around the reservoir, was a good twelve miles from Oakland. This was as close as Rosalind dared to be while telling her story to the press.

Ndidi set up her phone to record their conversation, and Rosalind began to answer her questions as they walked. The story slowly began to unspool from the compacted contours of Rosalind's mind. She began to explain things faster and faster, relieved to finally have someone to talk with. Even if it was a total stranger and a reporter from *The San Francisco Chronicle*, at that.

After half an hour, Ndidi clicked off the recording, saved it, and put her phone away. "You mentioned you have documentation…"

"Here." Rosalind pulled a thick, yellow envelope out of her backpack and handed it to her. "It's screenshots and time stamps of everything I found, along with each day's security reports. I've mapped out the discrepancies in yellow."

"And the recording you mentioned?"

Rosalind reached into the pocket of her jacket and extracted a stick drive. She handed it to Ndidi. "It's of my last conversation with Scott."

"Have you got a lawyer?" Ndidi asked, and Rosalind shook her head.

"Get one," she said. "This could break very quickly."

Ten minutes later, Rosalind got in her car and stared through the windshield. She began to shake uncontrollably as she considered what she had done. Then finally, mercifully, tears of relief started to roll down her face.

The future had just arrived.

Chapter Seventeen

Kate stared at her laptop, willing herself to write yet another short, clever email to her media contacts about Rendale Vineyards, makers of a high-end, oaked Viognier. "*Wine Spectator* calls it 'a class unto itself,'" she typed wearily. Suddenly, Kate stopped.

If she wasn't here, working in this quiet church classroom in Oakland, she would be...where exactly? In the family pub, toting plates loaded with Bernie's greasy fish and chips, or his leaden boxty? Kate sighed. She could see it now.

In the background would be the incessant whir and beep of video game terminals, with an abundance of ferns and cheap brass everywhere. She'd heard Da had done up the place.

Perhaps Kate wouldn't go home at all, once she landed back in Ireland. She was, after all, an independent woman now. Working for Mindy, her tyrannical ex-boss, had taught Kate what she was made of.

Now she knew how to find her way. She'd done exactly that in the ten months since she'd left her job and struck out on her own. And yet...how much could she actually have accomplished without Lizzy?

Lizzy had taken her in, given her endless love and support, connected her here and there, and even employed her when she needed it most. They were a good team. It was a simple fact.

Lizzy's natural enthusiasm lightened Kate's worrying and dithering. But Kate's attention to detail filled in the critical gaps around Lizzy's usual wild, seat-of-the pants approach. Like the time they cleaned up and painted the garage, and set up the now popular conversation corner. Even though Kate still worked for Mindy at that point, and Mindy had been actively trying to derail Lizzy and Tenika's garage.

It all happened in a single, action-packed weekend, fueled by coffee, inspiration, defiance, and ...yes...love.

Kate never would have taken on such a project. It would have seemed nothing less than impossible, but with Lizzy as the driver they simply flowed from one task to the next. And then, almost magically, it was done. Lizzy had even gotten Tenika so fired up, she personally power washed every inch of the floor until it gleamed.

It took everything the three of them had, but in the end, they did it. Then Tenika went home, and Lizzy and Kate collapsed, satisfied and exhausted, on the love seat together. Which was when everything began.

A bittersweet pang filled Kate as she remembered their first kiss.

She dismissed her thoughts and returned to the open email. The words swam in front of her. She so didn't want to be here, writing about white wine and awaiting an uncertain future. When she told the truth about it, she just wanted to be with Lizzy again. Recalling the past just brought up all the longing she'd been hiding from successfully until now.

Kate sat back and studied the poster hanging in front of her on the wall of the classroom. "Faith," it said in big, bold letters. Underneath was a quote from Voltaire. "Faith consists of believing when it is beyond the power of reason to believe." Kate closed her eyes in pain.

Lizzy always had that unreasonable reason to believe. That's what had gotten the two of them this far.

What was she doing, anyway?

She needed to call Lizzy right now.

*

Monroe gave a soft knock on Catalina's door, and waited. Now was as good a time as any to get her thoughts on the delicate matter of Kate and her romantic availability. Catalina would certainly be home. And most likely, she'd have some very good advice.

There was no reply.

Monroe leaned in, listening. There was no sound from inside the room. Monroe tapped again. "Hey there…" they said through the door. "Catalina?"

Again, stone cold silence.

"Huh." Monroe stood back and put hands on hips, assessing the situation. They'd already done a cursory search of the church.

Catalina wasn't in the study or the kitchen, or even the sanctuary, though she seldom spent time there. Monroe had half expected to smell pork tamales steaming when they got to the church, but everything was strangely quiet.

Monroe had assumed she was in her room, possibly taking an afternoon nap. But she wasn't, which was just plain odd. Now a surge of worry started in Monroe's gut. They pulled out their phone, and sent Catalina a text.

"Hi. I'm outside your door…u around?"

Monroe waited several moments but there was no reply, even though Catalina was usually a fast and ready texter.

Monroe debated what to do. Perhaps Catalina was out in the side yard, where she sometimes took the sun. The steady rain outside assured that wouldn't be happening today. Still, to be on the safe side, Monroe hurried down the stairs toward the kitchen. A moment later, they opened the side door and peered into the rain-soaked yard. There was no one there.

Now Monroe took the stairs two at a time, a rumble of panic rising in their gut. Something was definitely wrong. A moment later, Monroe knocked again more loudly on Catalina's door. Then they began to bang loudly, as fear took hold.

Gingerly, Monroe tried the doorknob to Catalina's room. It was unlocked. "Hey Cata—" Monroe began as they opened the door. But their words devolved into a low, guttural scream.

Catalina lay on the floor just inside the door. She appeared to be dead.

*

"I don't know. I just found her like that," Monroe repeated for the third time, now for the benefit of the Oakland Police Department. An officer stood in the kitchen, taking notes on a fat, well used pad.

Eleven minutes had gone by since Monroe called 911, and five since the EMT's arrived and set to work reviving Catalina. Miraculously, her heart was beating again even though it had completely stopped. She was still unconscious. It wasn't clear how long she'd been without a heartbeat.

Monroe watched as Catalina was hustled past her on a stretcher. Carefully, Catalina was lifted into an ambulance parked just past the kitchen door. Reverend Albiola climbed in beside her large, sheet covered body, a tense look on her face.

"Tell everyone what's going on," she called to Monroe as the ambulance door began to close.

"I will."

"And pray—*pray!*" the Reverend exhorted.

The ambulance took off, siren blaring, and Monroe turned back to the police officer. Monroe began to tell him what they knew about Catalina's next of kin, which was pretty much nothing. Kate now appeared in the kitchen doorway directly behind the officer.

Alarm was painted across Kate's face as she watched the unfolding scene. She and Monroe locked eyes, and instantly the shock and panic Monroe had been wading through morphed to a new emotion. Relief.

The officer's radio now sounded, and he turned aside for a moment.

Immediately, Monroe went to her. "Catalina's had a heart attack. Or a cardiac arrest, I guess. She's…it's critical." Monroe was trying not to shake. "The Reverend wants us to pray."

Kate nodded and slipped back through the door into the shadows. Monroe watched her head straight back to the sanctuary. Monroe longed to follow her, but now the officer stuck the radio back on his belt and resumed his questioning.

"What was your relationship to the deceased?"

Jesus. Have a little faith, Monroe thought. "She's not dead yet."

"Sorry—the person involved." The officer paused, but Monroe's focus was gone, trailing off down the hall after Kate.

"Ma'am?"

Monroe looked at the officer. "Not ma'am. I'm gender-queer. You can call me Monroe."

"Oh. Right." The officer looked slightly flustered. He made a note on his pad. Then once more he resumed the task at hand. "You were saying?"

*

Kate fell to her knees on the cold, stone floor of the sanctuary for the first time since she'd come into this church. She was overcome by an incredible sense of fragility. Not just her own, but everyone's. If there was ever a time to pray, it was most certainly now.

If Catalina could suddenly collapse—and even potentially die—then so could all of them. And of course, they would die sooner or later. But until now, that possibility always lived in the far off land of 'someday.' The sudden immediacy of death was breathtaking.

Kate closed her eyes and whispered a prayer for Catalina

to somehow survive this, and for her ailing heart to become well again. She prayed for Catalina to come back to Peace and Justice just as she had been before. Healthy and strong, once again making coffee and tamales, and dispensing her usual good advice.

Catalina's collapse just didn't seem possible. Yet, somewhere in the back of her mind, Kate knew this was exactly what would happen. The truth of Catalina's demise was just something she could feel.

It was, quite simply, her time.

Kate sat back on her heels and lowered her head as this awareness sifted through her consciousness. Fat tears landed on her arms and her jeans. Catalina couldn't die…she was too normal. Too strong. And she was too damn present to suddenly slip away and never return. She was also too important.

Maybe Kate was wrong. Maybe Catalina would actually survive and come back. She'd be weaker, perhaps, but filled with resolve to exercise and take better care of herself. Kate would even walk laps around the church with her if she needed her to.

Kate's thoughts hadn't yet circled back to the obvious. If Catalina did manage to survive, ICE would probably arrest her, most likely as she was leaving the hospital. One way or another, it was almost certain that Catalina would never return to the church.

Kate prayed for a long time, her knees growing numb on the cold stone of the church floor. But somehow, it felt right to be in pain and discomfort as her new friend, her dear friend, went through this ordeal. It felt like the least she could do.

A new thought struck her as Kate finally, creakily got up off the floor and lowered herself into a pew. She would not be able to visit Catalina in the hospital. She would need to depend on the Reverend, and even Monroe—perhaps even Lizzy—for updates and details of their visits.

That was assuming Catalina lived.

There was a sound now, and Kate turned around. Monroe was coming up the center aisle toward her, their face awash with tears. Kate stood. "What?"

"Catalina is…" Monroe began, but they couldn't finish. A sick feeling of dread rushed through Kate, and her brain suddenly lit up on high alert.

"She's dead," Kate said, and Monroe nodded.

Monroe stood there in front of Kate, tears running down their cheeks "A social worker from the hospital called. She had another cardiac in the ambulance. She…she didn't make it."

Kate made an involuntary sound, a swoon of grief. Monroe held out their arms, and she came into them. They stood there, holding each other and crying for a long time.

There was nothing else they could do.

*

Lizzy turned up the radio and hummed a little Al Green as she sped along 580 toward the church. The afternoon had been lit with possibilities. She even closed the garage early, and managed to get Kate an engagement ring. Well, okay—it was provisional. A small diamond set in rose gold, from a jeweler in the Laurel who said she could return it if she had to.

And Lizzy knew she might need to. It wasn't like Kate was thrilled about the prospect of getting married to her. Not yet, at least.

Somewhere between the lawyer's office and the garage, Lizzy found clarity. It occurred to her while she was sitting at a traffic light. The new attorney had been exactly right. It *was* up to her.

Lizzy could totally make things happen when she set her mind to it. All she'd needed was a nudge and a few instructions.

Lizzy turned up the radio. Now Al was singing about how loving his woman was what he ne-e—e—e-ded… 'cause he was still in love with her.

Just like Al, Lizzy needed this relationship. She *needed* it, with all her heart. Kate lit her entire life up in ways she'd never experienced before. And yes, okay, Lizzy knew she was a hard-core romantic, but still. Even Tenika couldn't fight the idea that they were solving an immigration problem with love.

She would indeed pop the question again, and this time she would do it right.

The glorious new fact was that there actually were options. Lizzy could see them now. She could probably talk the Reverend into giving them ten more months in the church. After all, it wasn't like she was sleeping on a pew. And if not, well…who knew? Maybe another sanctuary church in the Bay Area suddenly had room for Kate. Either way, Lizzy now had faith.

Somewhere along the way, Lizzy had also decided this was her last-ditch effort. Once she made her pitch to Kate to get married, then that was it. At that point, she'd leave Kate alone, satisfied she'd done what she could to help her stay. Then the fate of their relationship was no longer up to her and her efforts, and she could walk away in peace.

Lizzy pulled up to park in front of the church, turned off the truck, and set the brake. The ring box rattled around in the pocket of her jacket as she hurried up the main steps into the sanctuary. A surge of giddy excitement fluttered through her gut.

Rounding the corner from the vestibule, Lizzy strode along purposefully. But then she saw something that made her stop dead in her tracks.

Fifty yards in front of her, Kate and Monroe were locked in a tender embrace. Both of them were crying. More accurately, they were sobbing in each other's arms for all they were worth.

Lizzy stood stock-still for a moment, unsure what to make of the scene. She shifted uncomfortably from one foot to the next, trying to quell the vast demons of her imagination. Monroe and Kate continued to cry together, oblivious that she was standing there.

Finally, Lizzy cleared her throat.

Kate looked up and immediately released Monroe from her arms. Almost guiltily, Monroe glanced around and saw Lizzy. Then Monroe dropped into the pew beside them, and slumped dejectedly.

Kate meanwhile hurried toward Lizzy, arms outstretched. "Oh, Lizzy…thank God you're here."

"What happened? What's going on?" Lizzy asked, but Kate couldn't answer. Instead, she found her way into Lizzy's embrace. She pressed her face into Lizzy's jacket and began to cry once again in earnest.

They held on to each other for a long time. First for one minute, then two. Still Kate was unable to speak. Finally, Monroe stood up and walked toward them, wiping their face on their sleeve.

"Catalina's dead," Monroe said.

Lizzy looked up. "Wait—*what*? Catalina? *This* Catalina? *What the fuck?*"

"She collapsed less than an hour ago. Heart attack. Or cardiac arrest, actually. They took her to the hospital, and she died before she got there."

"Oh, *Jesus.*" Lizzy felt the power of the announcement down through her feet. Catalina, the friendly woman she'd chatted with a few times in the kitchen, was dead. It didn't seem possible.

Kate pulled back and looked up at Lizzy now. "She was just talking to me yesterday. She was just here. She was…"

"Alive," Monroe finished.

"I prayed for her, but…" Once again, Kate began to cry.

"Oh, babe." Lizzy's arms folded around Kate again, feeling a rush of tenderness coming from deep in her body. Right now, she just wanted to comfort her lover with every ounce of love she could muster. Lizzy was here for Kate, fully and completely, with a pull that had been written through time.

There was simply no other place Lizzy wanted to be.

"It's gonna be okay," she kept repeating into Kate's hair,

caressing her with strong arms. She kept planting small kisses along Kate's brow, as she dissolved further into Lizzy's embrace. Kate was crying more softly now, her face still buried in the large wet spot on Lizzy's canvas jacket.

Finally, Kate pulled back and sniffed, pushing the tears from her face. Lizzy pulled a worn blue bandanna from her pocket, and handed it to Kate.

"It's not okay, Lizzy. It's never going to be okay," Kate said. "Catalina's *dead*. She's not going to show up with tea in the morning, or give me good advice, or call me *flaquita*..." Kate began crying all over again. "She's just *gone.*"

"Let's sit," suggested Lizzy, gently steering Kate toward a pew behind them.

Now Lizzy's thoughts began racing about the larger implications of Catalina's sudden death. There would now be room for another sanctuary guest at the church. Room that Kate was uniquely poised to take advantage of.

Apparently, Kate had forgiven her, as well. Everything was suddenly moving forward again.

Lizzy shook her head, pushing these thoughts as far away as she could. This was totally not the time for all that. She just needed to sit with Kate right now. To hold her. To comfort her. To be with her. That was her sole job right now.

After a few moments, everything became still in the sanctuary. The three of them sat there, tied together in a quiet, unified shock. Lizzy thought of the engagement ring in its box, still taking up space in her pocket. The very idea of proposing to Kate, much as she had wanted to only moments earlier, now seemed entirely wrong.

Suddenly, everything had changed. Lizzy was not in control of this situation any more than she had ever been. She would simply have to just bide her time and see what happened next.

If there was to be a proposal, she would know exactly how to make it. And when.

Chapter Eighteen

Sally pulled Tenika's truck up to the pick up zone at SFO, scanning the spew of bleary travelers emerging from the terminal. A stream of people passed by, but none of them were Tenika or Delilah. Sally checked her phone again.

In baggage claim, it read.

They would be here in a few moments, presumably looking relaxed and happy and full of stories about their honeymoon. Then Sally would at least attempt to summarize everything that had been going on in Oakland since they left. It was a daunting task.

At the very least, she would attempt to be positive and upbeat about her and Frankie. But the wound of their fight was still fresh somehow, even though many days had passed. Never before had Sally been so angry for so long. The problem was the surge in her independence. It filled her with a fiery mojo she wasn't yet willing to part with. And frankly, it felt delicious.

Still, Sally was confused. Was she being too hard-core? Too judgmental? Exactly how long was she supposed to hole up in righteous anger? Part of her longed to call Frankie up and end the standoff. Watching her lover walk away from the front door that sad afternoon had been an exercise in extreme self-control. She'd never been here before, and she was beginning to doubt herself.

At least a dozen times, Sally picked up Frankie's lavender envelope intending to open it up and read it. And each time she put it back in its spot by the front door, not quite ready to capitulate. Because, of course, Sally knew what was in the letter.

It was an apology. Frankie had told her so herself, albeit through the front door. And how could Sally resist an apology? Every ounce of her tender, compassionate heart wanted her to read the letter, call Frankie up, and get back to being lovers.

She suspected Tenika and Delilah would tell her to do exactly that. Unless, of course, Tenika thought she never should have mentioned Rosalind's reading to Frankie in the first place. Perhaps the conversation would end with the fact that she blew her client's confidentiality.

Then there was the larger issue. Once she accepted Frankie's apology, wouldn't they still be fundamentally incompatible? Frankie was probably never going to get over her innate distrust of all things metaphysical. It just wasn't in her bones.

Shouldn't Sally just give up on Frankie? Even if it had felt so right, and so guided?

Now she spotted Tenika, moving fast through the crowd, trailed by Delilah. Tenika was waving and smiling, pulling a large suitcase on wheels. Behind her, Delilah wore an enormous floppy straw hat, presumably purchased in Belize, and some oversized shades. Her luggage was pure vintage, including a small, blue vanity case she carried primly in her hand.

Both of them looked happy and relaxed, as if a cloud of pheromones had followed them out the door. Sally hopped out and opened her arms for a hug. Tenika reached her first.

"Was it a great time?"

"It was a crazy crazy HELLA serious *excellent* time!" Tenika exulted. "Some big time fishing and snorkeling. I got in a shark tank—Delilah has it on video. *And* I'm thrilled to be back. I think I need a little tension," she joked as she threw their bags in the truck bed. "I missed it!"

"Thank you so much for coming to get us." Delilah gave Sally a hug, then she stopped and regarded her friend. "You okay, Sally?"

Sally sighed. "It's a long story. You driving, T?"

"Of course." Tenika took the keys and climbed in happily behind the wheel of her truck. They pulled into the slow-mo crawl of traffic leaving the airport.

"So, a lot has been happening," Sally began, not quite knowing where to begin.

"Uh oh," Tenika said. "Like good or bad a-lot-has-been-happening?"

"Well, you know…" Sally evaded.

Delilah leaned forward from the backseat of the truck. *"What* exactly?"

"Oh, it's nothing dramatic," Sally began. Yet it was dramatic—nearly all of it. Where on earth should she start?

Sally cleared her throat. It was best to stick with her own story, she decided. Delilah and T would hear everyone else's soon enough. "So Frankie and I broke up. Kind of."

T started in her seat, and she glanced over at her friend. *"Broke up?* What the hell happened?"

"Keep your eyes on the road, honey. What happened?" Delilah asked.

"It's my work," Sally sighed. "It's been a problem since day one. I told you about it."

"Come on! Seriously? What—your cop can't handle a little voodoo magic?"

"T…" Delilah's voice carried a low note of warning.

"All I'm saying is there are right brainers and left brainers."

Sally spoke up. "I made a mistake. I mean, *maybe* I made a mistake. At this point, I don't even know." She hesitated, almost afraid to share her story. Then she sat up a little straighter and took a breath. "So, here's the thing," Sally began. "I told Frankie about this reading I did for a woman in tech. I saw some really bad stuff connected to her job."

Tenika glanced at her. "How bad?"

"A mass shooting in Jack London Square. I mean, I got crystal clear details about it. So I told Frankie about it. I figured maybe she could help prevent it."

The three of them were silent for a moment.

"Then what happened?" Tenika asked.

"Frankie rolled her eyes and refused to help. She basically said no one would take me or her seriously, that my readings weren't real. That's when I got mad and left her in the middle of the Bay Trail. And basically, I haven't spoken to her since."

"Sally, Frankie was never going to be a big help with all of this," Delilah remarked.

"I guess not," Sally said. She let out a breath. It felt good to talk about things. "But let's just forget about it. It's over anyway. Tell me about your honeymoon."

Tenika looked over at her friend and shook her head. "Not so fast, girlfriend."

Delilah leaned in again from the back seat. "So have you talked since your fight?"

Sally sighed at the memory. "Frankie tried to apologize. A couple of times, actually. She's texted and called. She even put a love letter through the mail slot." Her voice trailed away as she stared out at the traffic on 101. "I just felt like I couldn't talk to her. Somehow I needed this to be right for once." She looked back at them. "Do you know what I mean?"

Delilah nodded. "I do. But Sally, maybe it's time to go talk it out with her."

"That or let it go once and for all," said Tenika.

"Here's the thing," Sally continued. "If we go right back to where we were, how do I know that she's ever going to take me seriously in the future? What if she never does? I mean, I'm not going to stop being a psychic."

Delilah leaned forward. "What was in the letter?"

"I don't know," Sally admitted. "I haven't read it."

"Oh, well…that's a different matter altogether," Tenika said. "You've got to read the letter, Sally. You can't waste a love letter. That's some serious shit."

"True," agreed Delilah. "At least read it. How long's it been since your fight?"

"I don't know…a week? Maybe more?"

"Honey, Frankie gets the point," Delilah said gently. "It sounds like she's trying."

Sally was silent for a moment as they drove along. This much was true. She thought back to a text Frankie had sent her only the day before.

Want to talk? I do, it said. At least Frankie wasn't giving up on them yet.

Yes, Sally realized. She actually did want to talk. The point had been made.

"Thanks, guys," she said. "I guess I'd better call Frankie. Somehow I just needed to talk it through with you." Sally shook her head. "You two have been seriously missed."

"What else has been going on?" Tenika asked. "Did Kate find a church?"

"Where do I begin?" Sally shook her head. "T, I'd advise you to get over to the garage as soon as you drop your bags. Lizzy needs to be talked off the proverbial ledge."

Tenika chuckled. "How did I know? Okay, sister. We got this." She glanced in the rear-view mirror at Delilah. "You with me, honey?"

Her new wife smiled at her from the backseat. "We're on it, babe."

Sally smiled and leaned back in her seat at the highway unwinding ahead. Relief was now officially at hand.

*

Tenika pulled up to the garage, and she and Delilah got out. The huge garage doors were down, but they could see lights on. Lizzy was apparently at work inside.

Tenika pushed the door open. "Lizzy? You here?"

Lizzy peered out from under an aging Toyota Camry that was up on the lift. "Hey, hey T! You're back!"

Lizzy tossed the caliper on the counter nearby and strode, beaming, toward her business partner. She opened her arms for a hug. "Man, you guys look great. Seriously, T, you should go on vacation more often. Actually, I take that back. Don't leave too often, okay?"

Lizzy hugged Delilah as Tenika laughed. "Don't worry. I hear all hell broke loose while we were gone."

"I guess you could say that." Lizzy gave a small embarrassed laugh. "Let's just say things have been moving along. Rapidly."

"That bad, huh?"

"Fucking horrific."

Delilah seated herself on the stool at the counter, getting ready to listen. "Details please."

"Where do I begin? That old client of ours, Monroe? They got Kate into sanctuary at Peace and Justice temporarily, which was amazing. But then, Kate went apeshit and stopped speaking to me."

Tenika and Delilah exchanged a glance. "Wait—Kate, too?" Tenika said.

Lizzy looked confused. "What do you mean?"

"Sally and—Frankie—oh, never mind," Delilah waved Lizzy forward. "Go on."

"So Kate got like…depressed? I don't really know. All I know was I was on her shit list. But I kept talking to this Mexican lady, Catalina, who was also in sanctuary there at the church, and she told me not to give up. So I went ahead and found another immigration lawyer anyway, who—"

Tenika stopped her. "Wait a minute. Back up. What do you mean *anyway?*"

"Oh …" Lizzy looked down, slightly abashed. "Well, when I was driving Kate to the church I gently suggested we get married so she could stay, and she was like no way in hell. She wanted to go the legal route, but her lawyer was doing literally nothing. I mean NOTHING. Right? So—"

Tenika closed her eyes and slowly shook her head. "Oh, Lizzy …"

Here it comes. Lizzy sighed.

"Lizzy Lizzy Lizzy," Tenika intoned. "What's it going to take? You can't rush this shit and get all up in people's business. Like I've told you. Am I right, honey?" Tenika glanced back at Delilah.

"You're totally right. Lizzy. Look, it sounds like Kate's just got a process she's in, and you have to respect it. You just do."

"But she was depressed! She wasn't getting out of bed. She was barely eating. And who knew how long she could even stay at the church, because technically—zoning and whatever—they could only take one sanctuary person. So she was basically sleeping in a storage room. Anyway…" Lizzy's voice dropped. "Everything just changed."

"How so?"

"The Mexican lady, Catalina? Well, she just had a heart attack and died." Lizzy shook her head. "I had a ring in my pocket, I was ready to propose…and boom…suddenly everything changed. So, I haven't proposed. Yet."

Tenika's brow now creased. "You had a *ring* in your pocket? *Seriously?*"

"Yeah," Lizzy said, putting her hands in her pockets. "The lawyer told me to marry Kate in the church as soon as possible. We just have to fill out a bunch of papers, then Kate only has to stay there for ten more months—"

"Wait a dang minute here, Lizzy. First of all, does Kate even know about this other lawyer?"

Lizzy shook her head silently, and Tenika rolled her eyes.

"First of all, somebody died, so have a little respect for the dead. Was Kate friends with the woman?"

Lizzy nodded. "Yeah," she said in a small voice. "Good friends. I know…I know. I'm sorry. I just wanted this to work out. Obviously, I can't go waltzing in there with a ring and propose."

"No, you sure as hell can't," Tenika agreed.

"But the good news is that Kate is actually speaking to me. She even let me comfort her. Then she made me go home."

"Okay. That's progress," Delilah said.

"Still," Lizzy said. "Now at least there's room for Kate to stay at the church."

Delilah sighed. "Oh, Lizzy," she said.

Tenika stood up. "You've got to stop, girlfriend. Just. Freaking. Stop. Let go. I know you're wired like a bulldog, but seriously, girl."

Lizzy sighed. "Yeah, I know."

The three women looked at each other. Delilah walked over to Lizzy now, and gave her a hug. "When you propose, it's got to be the right time," she said. "Just be patient a little longer, Lizzy. You'll get there."

"I know," Lizzy said. She smiled and shook her head. "It's incredibly sad…but it's weird. Because it's also wonderful."

"Sometimes that's the way life is," Tenika said.

"Think Catalina wanted Kate to marry you so she could get out of there?" Delilah asked.

Lizzy shrugged. "Maybe. She told me not to give up on Kate, even when Kate wasn't speaking to me. I kept leaving her notes and groceries and things. I just needed to…you know?"

"Yeah, I know." Tenika smiled. "That's love, sister. Right there."

"Keep the faith, Lizzy," Delilah added. "Your time will come."

Lizzy gave a bittersweet smile. Her friends were exactly right.

Chapter Nineteen

As night turned to day, the first trickles of light began to creep into the sanctuary. Putting one foot in front of the other, Kate walked its perimeter. It seemed all she was capable of in this moment.

She hadn't been able to sleep. It was as if her entire life had suddenly been dramatically, intrusively wrung out. All the old assumptions were now gone, replaced by a strange, murky new emptiness. Kate barely knew what to make of it.

Catalina would no longer sit with her for hours in the side garden, just talking about life, or fill the church with her laughter. And Kate would no longer lie in bed for hours on end, feeling sorry for herself for being caught in the system and hating her life.

She would no longer stare up at the church window looming over her bed in the cold stone gloom, or endlessly study the fading arrangement of fake lavender flowers that sat on her bureau. She would, instead, get her fucking shit together. For real.

Which is why Kate was now walking endless circles around the sanctuary. She'd been at it for close to an hour. What she needed more than anything in this moment was to move, to feel some kind of life pouring through her body again.

She needed to feel like herself once more.

For fifteen minutes in the middle of the night, Kate considered leaving the church. Just opening the door, sticking her hands in her pockets, and taking a walk through the nighttime mist for block after block. She craved the cool moisture on her face, and the feeling of the wind, and the sounds you could only hear outside—the cars, the distant sirens. The waking birds at dawn.

Kate even opened the side door and peered out into the night. The sidewalk was entirely empty, and the low ultraviolet hum of a street lamp was the only sound. Then she slowly closed the door again, aware that this would solve nothing, and even potentially get her held up at gunpoint. Which was possible, given the neighborhood the church was in.

No, Kate would walk inside her home. Her sanctuary. Her safe haven. And here she would come back to herself. She rounded the corner by the back pew, and stuck her hands in her pockets. Once again, her mind turned to Lizzy.

Lizzy.

The question was no longer one of if or even when. Now, the issue was how. Kate had not yet texted or called Lizzy because she wanted to get it right, this proposal. Catalina told her what she had to do, and do it she would. This was, indeed, a sacred moment.

Once again, Kate circled past the chancel, and for a moment she stopped. She looked at the altar spread before her, and the vast, creamy dome of light above it. Her gaze traveled far overhead to a round, stained glass window far up near the peak of the rafters. It was an image of Millet's *Sower.* The working farmer held out his hand as he walked, as if to scatter seeds.

Some seeds had surely been planted, she thought. And now they were beginning to grow.

Kate walked up to the altar and stood before it, contemplating the candles . She spotted a lighter tucked discreetly behind the chalice, and she picked it up. Kate ignited the lighter and touched the flame to the central candle. She doubted the Reverend Albiola would mind.

This was for Catalina, and it was lit with gratitude for all she had brought to her life. A few tears welled in Kate's eyes as she turned and walked down the steps to resume her walk. It was the least she could do.

Catalina was absolutely right. Yes, she would marry Lizzy. As soon as it was a reasonable hour, she would call her to the church, and she would propose.

It was time to get on with the business of life.

*

Monroe couldn't sleep. The replay of finding Catalina's lifeless body on the floor had seared itself into their imagination, and they saw it every time they closed their eyes. Just as they saw Kate's terrified, bewildered look, and Reverend Albiola climbing into the ambulance.

Monroe kept flashing on her worried face, and her words. *"And pray…pray!"*

A thousand images cascaded through Monroe's mind. The big, sheet-covered figure of Catalina, strapped into the yellow gurney. The blue gloves of the attendants pressing on her chest, cutting her clothing away, affixing IV's, and electroshocks. Their quiet but focused commands as they worked to start her heart again.

Through it all, Monroe had stood out in the hall trying to grasp that all of this was actually happening. It had been so quick; there'd been barely any time to process it. And then there was Kate, looming out of nowhere like a beautiful sylph, her reddish gold hair gleaming in the darkness. Then she disappeared again almost immediately.

Monroe rolled over and replayed the moment they hugged, and Kate's body pressed into their own. Kate had cried in great heaving sobs that overtook her just as Monroe's did. For moment after moment, they cried together in a heartbroken unison. Then Kate relaxed, loosening just a bit in Monroe's embrace.

Together, for just a short while, they had weathered something.

Suzanne Falter

But then, there was Lizzy, standing in the aisle. Of course, Lizzy would come at that exact moment. And yet, this, too, was perfect, for this was just what was meant to happen. Kate was Lizzy's woman, and that was that.

If Monroe had had any doubts, seeing Kate move toward Lizzy with utter and total relief painted across her face dispelled them all. This was love in motion. Monroe was somewhat awed by it.

Monroe watched that afternoon as Kate and Lizzy went into Kate's bedroom and closed the door, presumably to lie down together, to hold and comfort each other. To tell each other all they needed to say.

But then Lizzy left, not long after that. She seemed...neutral, really. Monroe looked up to see her pass. "Bye," was all she said. Her expression was intent, and Monroe had wondered what had happened between them. At any rate, Kate's door remained closed for the rest of the afternoon. It had been a devastating day.

Monroe sat up on the edge of the bed now, and considered getting up. Maybe even getting to the church early. It would probably feel good to finish another housecleaning project for the reverend, and there was always the perpetually leaking bathroom sink on the second floor.

Monroe stretched and moved toward the shower. Turning on the water, they stepped in a moment later to the comfort of hot water. Then they stood there for a moment, letting it pour over their body. Monroe's eyes closed, savoring the comfort of hot, soothing spray.

There might be another Kate out there, they thought. Somewhere, maybe even in Oakland, there had to be someone for them. Maybe she'd come at just the right time, and not a moment sooner.

This was now Monroe's new prayer.

*

Lizzy reached for her phone in the pre-dawn darkness. There was nothing.

No text. No calls. *Nada.*

Walking away from Kate the previous day had been one of the hardest things she'd ever done. Every fiber of her being called out for her to stay, to lie down on that lumpy Murphy bed and hold her lover tightly while she cried, all night if necessary. Even if it *was* against the church rules.

But Kate said she needed to be alone, just to process everything. So Lizzy went, even with a smile on her face. "Call me if you need anything, baby," she'd said from the door. "I love you."

"I love you, too," Kate had replied.

I love you, too.

Thank fucking God, Lizzy thought as she rolled on her back. The eternal spigot of love was back on in her life. But Kate had not called or texted. Now, strangely, it seemed okay. Fine, even. Lizzy's worrying mind was temporarily at rest.

Kate was doing her thing, and Lizzy was just loving her from a slight distance. It occurred to her now that this was exactly what needed to happen. The poor woman needed space. And she, herself, apparently needed another lesson in patience.

At this moment, it was time for Lizzy to focus on her own life. Particularly the backup of vehicles waiting for her attention at the garage. She and Tenika were still playing catch up after Tenika's vacation, and closing early hadn't helped a bit.

Lizzy pulled open a bureau drawer and extracted a t-shirt. It was a well-worn black Toots and the Maytals t-shirt she'd gotten long ago at the Ashby Flea Market. At the time, it cost all of a buck, and Lizzy loved it. Not only did it do the job at work, but also Lizzy actually was partial to Toots.

She put it on, then reached into the closet and pulled out some clean coveralls. Maybe it was a Toots and the Maytals kind of day, she thought. She could feel the slightest beginnings of positivity moving through her.

A few moments later, she was putting the finishing touches on her turkey sandwich for lunch when her phone chimed. It was a text from Kate. Lizzy's heart quickened as she read it.

Can you come to the church? Maybe now?

Lizzy threw the sandwich in her backpack, grabbed an apple and her water bottle, and headed out the door as quickly as she could. She was on her bike and sailing down the hill from her house in minutes flat.

As Lizzy rode over to the church, she contemplated the possibilities. Kate could be ready to talk things through. To explain to Lizzy just what had been going on that made it so hard to communicate. And this time Lizzy would listen. Really listen.

She wouldn't try to correct, convince, or nudge Kate in any particular direction. No, she'd just plain old be there for her.

On the other hand, maybe Kate wanted to talk about her grief. To share her memories of Catalina, whatever those might consist of. It was clear the two women had done a lot of talking.

Or…and here's where Lizzy's stomach tightened…Kate could have decided to go back to Ireland. To break up with her. To just do her future in an entirely different way. The sudden death of someone around you tended to do that to people. Mortality, and life purpose, and all kinds of big questions came up.

Briefly, it struck Lizzy that she'd left the engagement ring at home. She could practically hear Tenika whispering in her head.

You are seriously not going to need the ring.

Nor would she need to talk about the lawyer, or marriage, or any of the life-changing plans she'd been hatching. It was time to simply show up and be present. And listen.

That was it.

Lizzy smiled as she coasted down Castro Street toward the church. She was eager to see what lay ahead.

*

Lizzy knocked quietly on the side door. "Honey?" Then she knocked again a little more loudly, unsure if Kate was actually in her room.

A moment later Kate opened the door, and for a moment Lizzy was dazzled. Kate wore a simple black sweater and skirt, and she seemed somehow radiant. Plain gold hoops adorned her ears, and she looked remarkably at peace.

"Wow," Lizzy said as she paused. "You look beautiful."

"Hi." Kate leaned forward and kissed Lizzy on the mouth. The two of them lingered in another kiss.

"Can I just say I missed that?" Lizzy remarked as she came in. She dropped her backpack on the floor by the bed and sat down.

"I'm glad you're here."

"Me too. Is everything all right?"

Kate nodded and smiled. "Oh, it's better than all right. It's… well, we'll get to that. First, come with me." She held out her hand.

Rising, Lizzy took her hand and followed her out the door of her bedroom. "Where are we going?"

Kate smiled over her shoulder, "You'll see."

Kate slowed and took Lizzy's arm as they entered the side aisle of the sanctuary. The place was still dark as only a glimmer of daylight passed through the windows. Up on the altar a candle burned. "That's for Catalina," Kate remarked, and Lizzy nodded.

"Let's take a walk," Kate said, motioning to the aisle in front of them.

"Here, you mean?" Lizzy followed Kate's lead along the edge of the sanctuary as they walked beneath the windows.

"I'm not stepping foot outside of this church, darling. Not now at least," Kate remarked.

"Right."

"I've walked around this sanctuary for hours since yesterday. Probably lapped it a hundred, or even two hundred times," Kate said as they walked. "I just needed to get clear on things."

"I can imagine," Lizzy said.

"There is something I need to say to you."

Lizzy's heart quickened again; she was still unsure exactly what was happening. "Go on," she urged.

"I walked and walked, trying to get square with myself," Kate continued. "I kept trying to understand how Catalina could have just suddenly died, while I lived. And if I was going to be the one left behind, how was I going to proceed? What exactly was I supposed to do?"

Lizzy studied Kate as she spoke, her face luminous beside her. "Was I going to go back to Ireland? Because, believe me, I painted out that entire scenario in living color so many times in my head. Going back to the pub, and spending my days pulling pints. At times, it has seemed like the kindest thing."

Lizzy quelled her desire to comment. Instead, she walked on in silence beside her lover, their footsteps making the only sound.

"But no," Kate continued. "Leaving wasn't the answer. It wasn't ultimately kind to you or to me. And it certainly wasn't what I wanted. Quite the opposite, in fact. Mostly I just thought about what Catalina told me."

"What was that?"

Kate turned and looked at Lizzy intently. "She kept telling me to marry you. She said if she had anyone who loved her, she would have jumped at the chance. That it was crazy to give up on us…even if it didn't ultimately work out." They stopped now, before the chancel. "Catalina told me that the day before she died."

Lizzy was silent for a moment, absorbing all of this. "Wow," she said softly.

Kate held out her hand to Lizzy. "Come."

Lizzy took her hand and followed her up the steps toward the altar. They stopped in front of the candle flickering on the altar, and now Kate looked at her with great tenderness. She took both of Lizzy's hands in hers. "Lizzy, my love, I apologize for not being smarter, or wiser, or just better about all of this."

"Oh, Kate, it's really—" Lizzy began, but Kate held up her hand, silencing her.

"I apologize for not fully appreciating the incredible gift you are in my life," she continued. "You've taken such beautiful care of me, even when I wasn't speaking to you. Even when I was totally confused and depressed. And you've advocated for me again and again…getting me in here, for God's sake."

Kate shook her head as tears welled once again in her eyes. "I honestly don't know where I'd be without you. I'd be gone—that's where I'd be. And I am so grateful," she whispered. Tears began to slide down Kate's face.

Lizzy reddened. "Well …" she began. But then she quieted as she looked at Kate. Clearly Kate had something else to say.

Kate leaned forward and kissed Lizzy tenderly on the lips. Then she pulled back and looked at her. "Sweetheart, will you marry me?"

Now Lizzy could no longer hold back. Tears came into her own eyes. "Oh, Kate," she said. Then, in a sweep of grand passion, she took her lover in her arms and kissed her deeply. Their tongues intertwined as the purest love they'd ever known passed between them. Lizzy could feel the intensity, the joy, the connection circulating through her entire body as Kate kissed her back.

Now Lizzy looked into her partner's eyes. "Yes, yes, *YES!*" she exulted, and they both laughed. Then they kissed again, vibrating in the perfect ecstasy of the moment. For now, in an instant, Lizzy could see the grand perfect design before them.

The hesitation, the delays, the tension, the hard work of finding the church, and of being patient. All of it had led them to now, to this perfect moment.

"Whew!" Lizzy said, shaking her head. "I can't believe this!" she laughed. Then she gave Kate another squeeze as she rested her cheek against Lizzy's shoulder. "I was so worried about you."

"I know," Kate nodded. "Now we just have to worry about how to get married."

"I actually know something about that," Lizzy mentioned as they began to walk toward Kate's room. "But let's talk about it later." They stepped inside, and Lizzy glanced behind her as the door was closing.

If there ever was a time to make love it was now. There wasn't a soul in sight.

"Come here," Lizzy said, leading Kate to the bed. But Kate was already way ahead of her. Kneeling beside Lizzy, she kissed her and unzipped her coveralls, as Lizzy found her way inside Kate's skirt. Together they moved out of their clothes and beneath the covers with a rush of practiced grace.

Lizzy's hand found Kate's thigh—the softest thigh she'd ever felt, she thought. When her fingers slid down between her legs, it felt like a remarkable homecoming. This was, quite simply, where they belonged. Kate knew it, and she knew it.

The rest of the story had, indeed, begun.

Chapter Twenty

Rosalind waited outside the Auntie Anne's pretzel stand, scanning the Thursday afternoon crowd at the mall. It was almost entirely tourists, save for a few retirees out for a lunchtime shop with the girls. Folding her arms, she leaned against the wall by the kiosk and waited.

She wasn't quite sure why Ndidi wanted to meet with her, but she wasn't taking any chances. This time, she traveled into San Francisco for their meeting. Now that she'd basically walked out of True Wire, she had plenty of time on her hands. She hadn't been there since then, and had no intention of ever going back.

This was based on the advice of her new attorney, a freshly minted libel lawyer named Max whose rates were quite affordable. Max had already advised she pack her things, and get out of Oakland, in case harassment followed the news break.

Rosalind looked at her phone again. Ndidi was now fifteen minutes late, even though the *Chronicle*'s offices were only a few blocks away.

Suddenly, Ndidi appeared, cresting the top of the escalator. She was slightly breathless. "Hey! Sorry," she said as she reached Rosalind. "I was in a meeting when you texted back. Got over here as fast as I could."

"Do you want to take a walk?"

"Sure," Ndidi said. They began to make their way through the vast, shopping utopia of the Westfield mall. "Really, I just wanted to give you a heads-up that the story is breaking tomorrow. At least, I wanted to tell you the hack-free way. So thanks for coming in."

Rosalind's stomach gave a flip. "Okay…" she said, trying to keep her voice calm. Part of her had imagined all along that the *Chronicle* wouldn't actually run the story. Or if they did, it would be three inches long and buried deep in the business section.

Even when the photographer had appeared the day before at her apartment door, Rosalind had assumed nothing much would happen with the pictures. Until this moment, she had been fairly relaxed about the media coverage. It was amazing how powerful denial could be.

But now the whole damn thing was alarmingly real.

"Where will the article appear?" Rosalind asked.

"Oh, front page. It all checked out and then some. Your notes were excellent, and your recording, too. They were quoted extensively in the piece."

A surge of adrenaline zinged through Rosalind's body. Rosalind swallowed. "And the pictures?"

"Some nice ones. So yes, your photo's in it."

The front page, with extensive quotes. And her picture. Which also meant top of the newsfeed on the website. Her parents were going to have a heart attack. She could just see her father picking up the paper, reading the headline, and seeing her picture. And then doing a massive double take.

Then there was the furious image of Scott. And, undoubtedly, his team of lawyers. Scott, who'd taken to sending threatening texts since she'd disappeared on him. Suddenly Rosalind snapped out of denial.

Shit. She really did have to get out of here. Like…now.

"You lawyered up, right Rosalind? Cause they'll be coming for you, you can be damn sure."

Rosalind sighed. "I got the lawyer. And basically my office

still looks like I work there, but I'm not going back. I'll be fired immediately, I'm sure. Maybe I already am." She shrugged, despite her inner panic. "I'm prepared for that."

"And you're leaving town?"

Rosalind hesitated. "That part's trickier."

Ndidi looked at her curiously. "Can I help somehow?"

Rosalind smiled. "No, no, Ndidi...you've already helped me so much. I just have to get my act together about leaving. I'm not really sure where to go."

Ndidi hesitated. Then she stopped and touched Rosalind's arm. "You realize this is a very big deal, right?"

Rosalind nodded, trying not to betray the deep anxiety twisting in her gut.

"Maybe a getaway?" suggested Ndidi. "Go to Hawaii. It's only four hours by plane."

"I'll figure something out."

"Okay," Ndidi said, looking at Rosalind. She gave her a pat on the arm. "Take care of yourself."

"I will." Leaning over she gave the reporter a hug. Then she watched Ndidi head back down the escalator.

Her entire life was about to become unrecognizable.

*

Monroe contemplated the heap of clothing now piled on Catalina's bed. All of it would go to Goodwill, or the Salvation Army, or wherever the Reverend decided. Methodically, Monroe began folding each piece, and placing them in one of the large, black garbage bags that dotted the room.

There was the large lavender top with spriggy embroidered flowers around the neckline, and the blue and yellow Warriors hoodie Catalina had sometimes worn. *Curry 30*, it said on the back. Monroe folded up several generic looking blue and black skirts—Catalina had never been one to wear pants—along with two brown aprons bearing the name of her tamale truck.

Monroe stopped and studied them for a moment. *Los Tamales de Catalina...Deliciosos!* they said. Monroe put the two aprons aside. One to keep, and one for Kate.

This was what became of a life after you died, Monroe thought. Someone, perhaps even a relative stranger, would go through each item in your life, deciding how to get rid of it. Perhaps the most important things would just be thrown in the trash. It seemed grossly unfair...and yet, appropriate somehow. For in the end, all of it really was ephemera.

In Catalina's case, she had no next of kin in the States. By now her mother, an elderly woman living on the Mexican coast south of Tijuana, had been informed of her death, but she was too old to travel. Even if she could afford the one hundred and thirty dollars for a tourist visa, it was doubtful she could get past the increasingly stringent U.S. customs and border patrol.

For this reason, Reverend Albiola had spent a good part of the morning on the phone, arranging for Catalina's body to be shipped back home to Mexico.

The totality of Catalina's death was only now just sinking in. Monroe scooped up a jumble of shoes from the back of her closet and put them in the nearest bag, followed by a few polyester nightgowns, a well-worn lavender terry bathrobe, and the contents of her underwear and sock drawer.

Within minutes, the pile of clothing was gone, and the black garbage bags were now half full. Monroe surveyed the room, hands on hips. It had taken less than an hour to clear out Catalina's belongings. But that was life in sanctuary, Monroe figured. You didn't go out, so you needed less stuff.

Monroe now picked up a candle on Catalina's bedside. It was a tall, white pillar with an oval picture of an angel affixed to it. *Ángel de la Guarda* was written in a biblical-looking script on a golden streamer beneath the picture. Monroe picked up a prayer card beside it, written in both Spanish and English.

Sweet companion, do not forsake me. Guide me and guard me all my days to live my best, be my best, and give to others as you have guided me…

Monroe sighed and placed the card back on the table, contemplating its irony. Little good the guardian angel did this time. On the other hand, when it was your time…it was your time.

Monroe picked up the card again, and pocketed it.

As Monroe began to sweep the bedroom floor, those words stayed with them for a moment.

To live my best, be my best, and give to others as you have guided me…

This was Catalina at her essence. Her heart was big, and her intentions were always kind. It was an example to live by.

There was a knock on the door, and Monroe looked up. Kate was standing there. Monroe stopped for a moment, and took her in.

"Hi," Kate said gently. She didn't look tired or haggard, or even stressed. In fact, she looked strangely rejuvenated.

"Hey." In a surge of shyness, Monroe studied the floor. Picking up the broom, Monroe began to sweep in earnest.

"How's it going?" Kate asked.

"It's going." Monroe was afraid now to look at her. *Just keep your head down and keep busy.* They would simply sweep through this particular Kate encounter. It seemed the only way to manage.

"Yeah," Kate said, a bit sadly. She watched Monroe push the broom for a moment. Then Kate cleared her throat. "Monroe, I was wondering if I could ask you a question."

Monroe looked up.

"You see, I actually need a bit of help with something." Monroe studied Kate's beautiful face as Catalina's phrase resounded once more in their head.

…and give to others as you have guided me…

"What can I do for you, Kate?"

"Actually it's a bit of good news in the midst of the shite storm."

Monroe loved how Kate said 'shit.' *Shite.* It was so Irish. "And what would that be?"

"Lizzy and I have decided to get married."

The news was a punch in the gut for Monroe. They just looked at Kate in stunned silence for a moment, before they could recover enough to be gracious.

"Wow…that's…that's great!" Monroe finally said, forcing a smile.

"Thank you." Kate and Monroe gazed at each other, and for one moment, Monroe entertained an irresistible thought. That they might tell Kate they loved her. Just once. Before the deed was done.

For Monroe knew now, that they most certainly did love Kate. Monroe pushed the thought to the furthest reaches of their mind.

Monroe focused once again on Kate's request. "You were saying?"

"I was wondering. Can Lizzy and I get married in the church?"

"Oh…well, yeah. Sure. Not on a Sunday morning, of course, but some other time."

"We were thinking tomorrow, or maybe the next day? As soon as possible, really. We can get a marriage license tomorrow."

Naturally. Why not marry Lizzy in a rush of wild, uncontrolled passion?

"We'll be happy to pay the fees," Kate continued evenly. "Perhaps Reverend Albiola could do the ceremony?"

Monroe nodded. "We need to get with her on dates. We can go talk to her right now. But, Kate, wait."

Kate turned to her, her face lit with the first smile Monroe had seen in days. "Here," Monroe said, handing the apron over to her. "Thought you might want this."

Kate took Catalina's apron and studied it for a moment, as another look of bittersweet sadness passed across her face. Tenderly, she folded it in her arms. "That is really thoughtful," she said. "Thank you, Monroe."

Then leaning over, she gave Monroe a soft kiss on their cheek. "You have been a truly good friend to me," she said. "I appreciate it."

Monroe just nodded as a flush of warmth flooded their body. Closing their eyes, Monroe took a deep breath.

The chance to give to others was already here.

*

Rosalind opened the door to Desire's Magical Garden, and it gave its customary tinkle of bells as she entered. "Hello there," said the owner. She was standing in front of an opened jewelry case with a small, pink feather duster in hand. Desire closed the case and put the duster down.

"How've you been?" she asked with a smile.

Inexplicably, Rosalind felt a sudden sweep of relief, and she smiled back at Desire. It wasn't as if she thought of Desire's Magical Garden as some sort of ersatz home. In fact, she'd barely thought of the store much at all, except for just now on her BART ride back from San Francisco.

As they passed through the long, dark rumble of the tunnel between the city and Oakland, it occurred to her. Rosalind needed to know more about her circumstances. And she *could* know more. There actually was a way. That much had been proven.

"Is Sally here? I was hoping to get another reading?"

"Sally's having her lunch in the back. Let me ask her." Desire disappeared through the velvet curtains behind her.

Almost immediately, she returned with Sally, who seemed excited to see her. "Hey, Rosalind!"

"Good timing," Desire remarked as she returned to her dusting.

Sally walked around the counter and gave Rosalind a brief, unexpected hug. "I'm so glad you came by," she said.

Stiffly, Rosalind hugged her back. "I totally didn't mean to interrupt your lunch."

"Oh, lunch can wait," Sally smiled. "Let's do another reading right now."

A moment later, they were seated once again at the small, round table, as Rosalind picked out a handful of cards and gave them to Sally. Thoughtfully, she began to lay out the cards, face down, on the velvet tablecloth.

"So what's on your mind, Rosalind? What brings you in today?"

Rosalind exhaled and felt her shoulders drop a few inches. "There's just a lot happening. A serious amount of stuff. I need some answers. But then, I guess that's what everyone says."

"Actually, I've been thinking about you," Sally admitted. "Wondering how your big challenge is going."

Rosalind gave a long, slow exhale. "That's why I'm here. I need to know more." She looked down at the table. "I'm almost afraid to learn more. But I figured it might be a good idea."

"Okay." Sally began laying the cards out on the table. "Interesting," she said, peering down at the first ones she turned over. "Perhaps you've been feeling a little lost?"

"How do you mean?"

"Disconnected from yourself…from your intuition or guidance. Just not knowing where to turn or what to do." Sally looked up and studied her for a moment. "Athena is reversed here. Are you avoiding something?"

The reversed card before Rosalind was of a dark-haired goddess, standing before a snowy owl in the moonlight. The message was one of fortitude—relying on your inner wisdom, even when it required you to go deep.

Rosalind seemed lost in thought for a moment. "Yeah," she

finally said. "I suppose there are some things I'm avoiding right now."

"Like?"

Rosalind looked sideways and shifted in her seat. "I can't say exactly what's happening, but basically, I need to get out of town."

Sally turned over another card. It was Cordelia. "Great. So here's a direct message to get outside. Get by the water, if you can. Oh—and look at this," Sally said as she turned the card next to it.

It was Nematoma, the goddess of sacred spaces. "See, that's just what I was thinking," Sally continued. "A few hours to the north, up in Lake County, is a hot springs resort called Harbin. The place burned to the ground in a wildfire several years ago, but now it's been restored. The pools and springs are open again. It's a truly gentle place in nature, just as it has always been and always will be, no matter what happens."

"Nematoma is inviting you to visit a sacred space," Sally added. "That's exactly what Harbin is. I think you should get up there as soon as you can."

"Interesting," Rosalind murmured. She'd never heard of Harbin, and she'd never been to a California hot spring. She would Google it.

"What else?" she asked.

"Brigit is telling you not to back down. Is there something you're wavering about right now?"

"Well, not really. I've done everything I can. But it might become challenging."

"This is your exhortation to proceed in due diligence. Calmly. Bravely. Continuing to do the right thing. You've got this, Rosalind." Sally pulled a few more cards and laid them out between them.

"And look at this—wow. Guinevere." She smiled up at Rosalind. "True love, even. Just part of the quantum change that's going on right now. It's a big time for you. But it's also an important one. A critical time, even…"

Rosalind cautioned herself. *Take these cards with a grain of salt. As ever.* True love was totally not top of her mind right now, no matter what Sally saw.

Sally closed her eyes. "Here's the thing. You have to be open and accepting, of other people and their differences. And you have to honor your own instincts and quirks. Just follow that ever-abundant stream of love that surrounds you, Rosalind. You know what I'm talking about because you've felt it. Even if it has surprised you at times."

Sally opened her eyes and looked directly at Rosalind. "No judgments," she concluded. "Just love."

"Okay," Rosalind said softly. She knew exactly what Sally was referring to. *No judgments against anyone else. But most especially, no judgments against herself.*

"It's a beautiful path, full of power, and possibility, and challenge. But you can handle it. You really, truly can." Sally sat back and smiled at Rosalind. "I think you're going to be just fine."

And Rosalind smiled back. She hoped to God Sally was right.

*

Kate opened the side door and let Lizzy in.

"Hey!" Lizzy leaned over and gave her a kiss. "You ready to do this thing?"

Kate took a big breath and nodded. "I am. I'm bloody terrified, so let's just get on with it before I get too scared." Getting married required they both show up several blocks away at the Office of the Clerk-Recorder to file their papers.

"You're not scared to—"

"To get the marriage license, no love," Kate said with a smile. She gave her lover a hug. "Not at all. I'm thrilled, I've told you that. I'm just scared about *them*." Kate nodded in the general vicinity of any ICE agents who might be lingering outside.

Lizzy wrapped her arms around Kate. "Don't worry, babe. There isn't a soul out there right now, except some homeless guy sitting on a spackle bucket with a sign. Anyway, I have a surprise for you."

Kate looked at her curiously. "What?"

Lizzy gave a grin of satisfaction. "Frankie's meeting us here in one of the SFPD patrol cars. She's giving us a police escort. She might even escort us inside if we ask nicely."

Kate smiled and shook her head. "Lizzy! You are too much."

"I figured the occasion called for a little drama. Anyway, Frankie's ICE contact says they're not even monitoring you right now. They're understaffed, just like everything else in Oakland."

"Seriously?"

Lizzy nodded. "Yep. You're perfectly safe."

Kate reached up and kissed Lizzy, this time lingering as their mouths moved together and their tongues found each other. It was a deep kiss—a real kiss. An honest, enduring love sort of kiss. "Thank you, honey," she said.

"Happy to do it, believe me." Lizzy's phone gave a small chime. "Cool. Frankie's here."

Lizzy opened the door, and Kate followed her out, blinking in the sunshine. She glanced around for a moment, getting her bearings, as if she'd been at sea for a long, long time and was newly returned to dry land. Then hurrying, Kate moved toward the waiting police car as Frankie got out and opened the door.

"Hey, lovebirds," she called.

Kate smiled up at Frankie. "Thank you so much, Frankie. You are amazing."

"Least I can do."

They took off on the five-minute ride. It was time to make their marriage a reality.

Chapter Twenty-One

Folding her arms across her chest, Frankie leaned back in her seat on the BART and did her best not to doze. The traffic gods had been with her as she made her way back across the Bay Bridge with the patrol car. It wasn't yet eleven, and the entire deed was done.

She'd even slipped the squad car back into its parking spot without the Lieutenant noticing. It had been a good strategy to take number forty three, the old clunker nobody wanted.

And it had been entirely worth it just to see the looks on Kate's and Lizzy's faces as they signed the papers. As she stood there, hands folded and patiently waiting, it occurred to Frankie. This was what she wanted, too.

To be held, and understood, and seen…to be loved. Pure and simple. Lizzy signed the papers, then Kate signed them, and they just looked so damned happy. Frankie smiled as she replayed the scene in her mind. Those two were clearly meant for each other. It was probably the nicest moment she'd ever witnessed in a county office.

Frankie glanced now at the person next to her, an older, silver-haired woman reading the front page of the *Chronicle*. Out of habit, Frankie's eye now glanced across the headlines on the newspaper beside her. As she did, she saw something that made her suddenly sit up.

"Local Tech Consultants Implicated in Jack London Square Terror Plot," it said.

Peering a little more closely, Frankie did her best to read the beginning of the article discreetly. *This could have been Sally's terror plot,* she thought to herself. Except for the fact that Sally's apparent 'vision' was just a vision.

Still, Frankie couldn't help herself. She read over the woman's shoulder, peering closer and closer as the facts laid themselves out, one by one.

The tech firm monitored fake news on massive social media sites. *Check.* The attack was supposed to happen at a rally in Jack London Square. *Check.* Hard drives seized from the offices showed they'd colluded with at least two foreign governments to disseminate fake news about the rally. *Check.* The company cleared and approved the very news they were supposed to be detecting and removing. *Check.*

Then this: The FBI had arrested two men involved in the event who had written extensively online about wanting to kill people at the rally. Frankie looked up in mild shock. This most definitely was Sally's vision.

The fucker was actually true.

Now Frankie peered even more closely at the article, until the woman folded down her paper and looked at her pointedly. "May I help you?" she asked.

"I'm just…sorry—that article…I was just interested…" Frankie sputtered.

Rolling her eyes, the woman handed the folded paper over to Frankie. "Here. Just take it."

Instead of protesting, Frankie took the newspaper. "Thank you," she mumbled. "Sorry." Frankie's eyes moved fast across the article one more time, scanning for anything that might disprove the rightness of Sally's vision. But it was all there.

Every last detail of the article lined up with what Sally had described. Frankie thought back to the moment when Sally had gently tried to share her vision with Frankie, and how hesitantly and vulnerably her words had come out. Even though she knew how Frankie would react.

Hell, even the FBI had gotten involved. A pang of remorse sank through Frankie's body like a ton of bricks. She stared out the window as BART pulled into the 12th Street Station.

She had totally and completely fucked up.

Not only had she been undeniably wrong, her now former girlfriend had been extremely right. She'd even asked Frankie to help her, and Frankie had been cocky enough to refuse. What, if anything, could she do to make this right?

Frankie got off at the next BART station, ready to meet her destiny.

It was time for the walk of shame, straight to Sally's house.

*

Stirring a little honey into her tea, Sally sat down at the table and opened her laptop to check her emails. Bright, late morning light filled her kitchen. The day had begun sweetly enough. Her guides had been there, whispering in her ear as she woke up.

Time to call Frankie, they'd said. She could feel the ethereal rightness of this in every fiber of her being. She simply had to get herself to open the lavender letter still sitting on the table in the entryway. Then she would call.

As Delilah had said, the point had been made. It was time to move forward.

Sally scanned her emails, looking for anything of interest. There was a forwarded message from Desire near the top. *From your client*, read the subject.

"Thought Sally might find this interesting," Rosalind had written. What followed was a link to an article in the *San Francisco Chronicle*.

Sally clicked on it and began to read. Immediately she noticed Rosalind's picture.

Rosalind was shown sitting on a couch with a tense look on her face. *Tech whistle-blower Rosalind Choi's surveillance and testimony exposed True Wire's efforts to propagate fake news on behalf of two foreign governments planning Bay Area terror attacks.*

All assets have been seized and the two principals of the company, including the owner, M. Scott Berring, are currently being held without bail. Charges are pending.

Sally sat back and stared at the news story on her computer as a quiet feeling of awe filled her body. This was her vision. It was all here. Leaning in to the screen, she re-read what she'd just read once more, as if it might have been an illusion.

But it wasn't. It was most definitely true.

Sadly now, Sally thought of Frankie. Frankie who was so filled with doubt, who rolled her eyes at the merest suggestion that her work wasn't all fantasy, smoke and mirrors.

And yet, it wasn't. If there ever was proof of that, here it was. Still, Sally did not feel vindicated, nor did she feel triumphant in that moment. Instead, she felt tender.

She knew she would never dissuade the Frankies of the world from having their beliefs, nor could she judge them. Instead, Sally's sole job was to accept them. And to try to understand them. For Frankie needed her beliefs, just like Sally needed her own.

The thing that filled her heart now was an insistent longing. She wanted to call Frankie up and share this with her right now. She wanted just to have a conversation together, to be like they once were.

Sally got up and hurried to the front door of the apartment. Picking up Frankie's lavender envelope, she slipped a finger under the flap and tore it open. Then she removed the letter and began to read. Frankie's blocky handwriting as it filled the page.

Sally, I am sorry, it began.

You had every right to ride away from me that day for my completely inappropriate, clueless comments about your work. Sometimes I feel like I'm learning from you, one date at a time, how to be a better person. And it's definitely a work in progress!

The thought that I hurt you has pushed me to a cold, sad, lonely place I never want to visit again. Please accept my apology.

You are an incredible woman, Sally, and I'm blessed to have known you and loved you. For what it's worth, I am most definitely still in love with you, and my life is much, much better when you are in it. I don't want to lose you.

Please tell me how I can make this up to you. Can we try again?

Frankie

Sally put the letter down, and an involuntary smile filled her whole being. Now she saw that Frankie understood something fundamental. Every relationship was a work in progress…just as every person was, too.

Yes, she would take Frankie back. And yes, they would work on things together. And yes, she would love Frankie just as much as she had from the very beginning. For that, most certainly, was their path. There was simply no other choice.

Walking fast, Sally headed back to the kitchen and picked up her phone from the counter. Quickly, she called Frankie but there was no answer. She was working, most likely. Though now, Sally realized with a pang, she no longer knew Frankie's work schedule.

Sally put the phone down and stood there for a moment,

assessing what to do next. Her eye fell on Frankie's love letter, lying open on the table. She picked it up.

What must it have taken for Frankie to write this?

Sally was re-reading it for the third time when the doorbell rang. Holding the letter in her hand, she went to the door, still caught in the thrall of the love that was pouring off the page.

Sally opened the door. Frankie was standing there with an enormous bouquet of white roses.

"Hi," she said. Her expression was a little tentative, as if she wasn't quite sure what to expect.

"Oh, honey," Sally said, as she dove into Frankie's arms. She kissed Frankie so hard she dropped the bouquet. "Hey!" Frankie laughed.

"Yes, I want to try again. Yes, I love you, too. Yes...to all of it!" Sally declared. Then pulling Frankie inside, she shut the door.

Now, the two of them began kissing again, this time more ardently. "I'm so sorry," Frankie kept saying, but Sally's kisses finally silenced her. "Come on," Sally said, tugging her toward the bedroom. "There isn't a soul home but you and me."

"The flowers?" Frankie asked.

Sally smiled. "Oops, sorry." Quickly, she opened the door, grabbed the bouquet, and marched it into the house.

"You...in the bedroom. Now," Sally said, pointing the way. Frankie laughed and did as directed, making her way to Sally's bed. A moment later, Sally appeared in the bedroom doorway. She was utterly naked and holding the vase of roses in front of her.

"This is for both of us," Sally said, "because I owe you an apology, too." Sally put down the roses and sat down on the edge of the bed. "I should have read your letter much, much sooner... but I just opened it," she admitted.

"You just read my letter now?"

"I know," Sally sighed. "I'm really sorry." She lay down beside Frankie. "I don't know if this makes sense, but I think we needed to have this fight." She ran her hand down Frankie's chest, tracing the space between her breasts. "I needed to know that I could walk away and really mean it. I needed to draw a line. So it turned out to be perfect, what you said to me."

Frankie grimaced, "Actually, no, sweetheart. It wasn't. No one ever needs to be an asshole. Or an idiot, as it turns out. You were completely right."

Sally smiled. "You saw the article this morning?"

"I practically ripped it out of this poor woman's hands on the BART. And yeah, I read every word. I mean…Jesus, Sally. That's pretty impressive."

"Oh, Frankie! It's not my gift—I've told you that. It just passes through me."

"Yeah, yeah, whatever. Sally, you're good. You're *seriously* good. Like you're a genius at this psychic thing. And I get it. I really, truly get it. And, honey?" Frankie took Sally's hand. "I will never, ever be critical of your work again. I swear it."

Sally smiled as the pure rightness of the moment passed through her. This was what she'd been longing for, pure and simple.

"Thank you," she said quietly, coming in for a kiss.

Love was most definitely back in town.

*

Rosalind gripped the steering wheel a little more tightly as she swung into the inner lane. The Bay glistened on both sides of the Richmond Bridge as she sped across it toward 101 North. The day was sparkling. The water was a brilliant aqua tinged with green, and Mount Tamalpais rose on the horizon. The air was lit with possibility.

Rosalind felt as if she were driving away from her entire past. She was leaving it all behind—the toxic workplace, the oppressive parents, the severe workaholic fervor. The aching isolation and loneliness. And the crazy shame that had locked all of it in place for so many years.

Rosalind was done with all of it, set free by her own redemption. Nowhere would there be a shadow in her life anymore. She was going to create an entirely new everything, beginning right here and right now.

Of course, she had no idea what this would include, or even how it would even take shape. She just knew that going to Harbin Hot Springs was the first step. And an outrageous step it was.

How likely was it that she, Rosalind, would hang out in a clothing optional resort? But then that's what this new life required. Bold, breathtaking action, the kind she'd never considered before.

And another thing. She was going to come out. If her parents never spoke to her again, then so be it. It was time. Rosalind simply couldn't deny who she was for one more moment.

Happily, she rounded the curve past San Quentin. She glanced back at the prison in her rear-view mirror, with its bleak watchtower and it banks of razor wire.

Gone gone gone, she wanted to sing. *All of it gone.*

There was only her future, shining, just ahead.

Chapter Twenty-Two

Kate turned and examined herself in the full-length mirror. "What do you think?"

"Amazing," Delilah said. "And if you wore jeans, that would be okay, too. I mean…given the circumstances."

There were only a few minutes left before the wedding ceremony was scheduled to begin downstairs. They'd had exactly twenty-four hours to put together the entire event, which included moving Kate into what had once been Catalina's room, her new sanctuary residence.

Kate smiled. "Wear jeans to my own wedding? Certainly not." The blue dress had been seen before, but it was a personal favorite of Lizzy's.

"Look. I found this in here," she said, showing Delilah the tagua nut bracelet on her wrist. The large nuts were smooth, thick, and ivory colored, and they circled her arm with authority. "It was on the floor of the closet. I think it must have been Catalina's." Kate gave a bittersweet smile. "A remembrance," she said.

Delilah nodded, "It's beautiful," she said, giving her friend a consoling stroke on the back. Then she took Kate's arm. "Everyone's waiting."

Kate took a deep breath. "All right," she said. Delilah handed her the single long stem, white rose she'd picked out for her. The two women smiled at each other.

They entered the sanctuary a few moments later. Kate gazed up the aisle of this church where so much had happened in such a short time. There was a knot of people seated in the very front pews. Reverend Albiola stood in the chancel in her purple robe, and she was beaming at Kate. Next to her stood Lizzy in a gray suit with a lavender shirt, open at the collar.

Tenika had taken Lizzy out to buy it the previous evening, and she looked especially sharp. Now Tenika stood beside her in a black suit with an orange, button-down shirt and a bolo tie. She was ready to provide the ring at just the right moment. Lizzy had an expression of total bliss on her face as she eyed Kate at the back of the sanctuary.

Frankie hurried up the side aisle and slipped into the front pew beside Sally as Monroe began to play Pachelbel's *Canon*. This was Kate's cue to begin. Delilah turned and smiled at her, and Kate gave her a nod.

"Go ahead," she said.

Delilah began to process slowly up the aisle, then Kate followed. Her heart was practically beating out of her chest as she walked toward the beaming reverend up ahead.

This was it, she thought. Finally she was delivered from her own sad, closed, hopeless state of mind. And from her dithering, and her indecision, and her fear. But then, it was always somehow in the plan that she and Lizzy marry. At least it was never *not* in the plan.

Kate had realized this not long after they met, on a particular evening when the two of them walked along the beach near Goat Rock, up on the Sonoma Coast.

On that evening, as the achingly cold Pacific pushed in around their ankles, making their pant legs wet, and the sky glowed with iridescent streaks of purple and pink, she knew. Just as Lizzy knew. This was a great love, whether she surrendered to it or not. It had always been and always would be.

It was up to Kate to seize the moment, to move toward it.

To finally let go and trust. And so...here she was. Trusting, at last.

Kate reached Lizzy's side and they smiled at each other. "Oh, honey," Lizzy said, and tears sprang into Kate's eyes. She wiped them away as she laughed a little, embarrassed.

The Reverend held out her arms as if to embrace the entire sanctuary. "Oh happy day!" she exulted. And everyone there spontaneously applauded and cheered.

The service began with a prayer for the dead, most especially for Catalina, inviting their spirits to join in the festivities. A sugar skull for Catalina had been placed on the altar along with a plate of tamales purchased from a nearby food truck and a bouquet of orange marigolds.

Everyone had a small part to play. Frankie read a poem by E E Cummings, and Sally quoted Buddha and Pema Chödrön. Delilah took Kate's single white rose as the minister asked Lizzy and Kate to join hands. And as she began leading them through their marriage vows, a single shaft of light came pouring through the tall church windows of the sanctuary, piercing the afternoon winter gloom.

It was in that shaft of light that Tenika handed Lizzy the ring, and Lizzy placed it on Kate's finger, saying, "With this ring, I marry you. For better, for worse, in sickness and in health, until death do us part." A moment later, Kate was making the same vows, sliding a similar gold band on Lizzy's finger.

The Reverend then held up her arms jubilantly. "I now present, with great, great joy, Lizzy and Kate. Spouses for life!"

This was the moment when Monroe stood up beside the piano, and simply said, "I wrote this for Kate...and for Lizzy." Then they began to play sweet, life-affirming music that filled up the sanctuary, rising to the rafters. Monroe played on and on, hitting the notes for all they were worth, a look of pure rapture on their face.

Lizzy and Kate kissed then, as all the barriers came down and, once again, they were truly united.

In love forever. Just as it was always meant to be.

About Suzanne Falter

Suzanne Falter is an author, speaker, blogger and podcaster who has published both fiction and non-fiction, as well as essays. Her queer fiction titles include the funny romantic suspense series Transformed. She also writes and speaks about self-care and the transformational healing of crisis, especially in her own life after the death of her daughter Teal. Her non-fiction books include *The Extremely Busy Woman's Guide to Self-Care, How Much Joy Can You Stand?* and *Surrendering to Joy*. Suzanne's essays have appeared in *O Magazine, The New York Times, Elephant Journal,* and *Thrive Global* among others. Her free flash fiction can be found at www.suzannefalterfiction.com, as well as on Facebook, Twitter, YouTube, and Pinterest. She lives with her wife in the San Francisco Bay Area.

Also by Suzanne Falter

Fiction
Oaktown Girls series
Driven
Committed
Destined
Revealed

Transformed: San Francisco
Transformed: Paris
Transformed: POTUS
(All titles by Suzanne Falter & Jack Harvey)

Non-Fiction
The Extremely Busy Woman's Guide to Self-Care
The Joy of Letting Go
Surrendering to Joy
How Much Joy Can You Stand?
Living Your Joy

Thank you to the supportive staff of Raven's Wing Magical Co. for providing the metaphysical information we needed.

Thanks for ideas and information as well from PSM.

Many thanks to Angelica Guerrero for the excellent tamales tips and accuracy read.

Thank you as ever to my crack production team, Danielle Hartman Acee, Gillian Rodgerson and our cover artist, Caroline Manchoulas.

Finally, thank you, Jack Harvey for making this series possible.

www.ingramcontent.com/pod-product-compliance
Lightning Source LLC
Chambersburg PA
CBHW020408210626
46816CB00006BB/2179